Smart, cool, ~~...~~ f his league

How often had Nick reminded himself of this, and why in hell did he want to kiss Cinnamon more than ever?

Nick studied her face openly, letting her see his interest.

This time she didn't look away. Her lips parted a fraction, and a rush of breath shot between them. Nick recognized those signals, knew if he moved closer, leaned down and kissed her, she wouldn't stop him. She'd kiss him back.

That scared him. Getting involved with Cinnamon Smith was dangerous. Crazy, even. Not an option.

Clearing his throat, he backed away. "I'll get my coffee now. And you ought to take that beach walk."

"Right. I'll go upstairs and grab my jacket." Cheeks flaming, she rushed toward the stairs.

As soon as she disappeared, Nick gave his brow a mental swipe and headed for the kitchen. He'd avoided kissing her. Barely.

Dear Reader,

Several years ago my husband and I spent Fourth of July in Bandon, Oregon, a tiny seaside town. The bed-and-breakfast we chose delighted us, and not only for its oceanside location and cozy, comfortable rooms. Shirley Chalupa, the personality-plus proprietress, entertained us with wonderful stories and fed us generously. I swear we gained ten pounds from those mouthwatering breakfasts. The town intrigued me, and I knew I had to set a series of stories on the Oregon coast.

Cranberry, Oregon, is a fictional seaside town, and so is the Oceanside Bed and Breakfast. But Stumpy and Stubby are real seagulls, coddled and fed by Shirley just as Fran spoils them in the book.

The love story between Nick and Cinnamon comes straight out of my imagination. I hope you fall in love with Nick as I did. The man is a true hero with a secret that darkens his life and forces him to hold his feelings in check. Until he meets the lovely, educated Cinnamon, who... well, you'll find out soon enough.

I hope you enjoy the first book of this three-book series. Write and let me know what you think of Cranberry, Nick and Cinnamon. You can reach me c/o P.O. Box 25003, Seattle WA 98165-1903 or e-mail me at ATROTH@comcast.net. Also, please visit my Web site at www.annroth.net, where you'll get the latest news as well as a delicious recipe of the month. And don't forget the contest. Enter to win a free book!

Sincerely yours, and happy reading!

Ann Roth

The Man She'll Marry

ANN ROTH

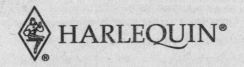

HARLEQUIN®

TORONTO • NEW YORK • LONDON
AMSTERDAM • PARIS • SYDNEY • HAMBURG
STOCKHOLM • ATHENS • TOKYO • MILAN • MADRID
PRAGUE • WARSAW • BUDAPEST • AUCKLAND

ISBN 0-373-75124-9

THE MAN SHE'LL MARRY

Copyright © 2006 by Ann Schuessler.

This edition published by arrangement with Harlequin Books S.A.

www.eHarlequin.com

Printed in U.S.A.

To Shirley Chalupa, bed-and-breakfast goddess
of the Oregon Coast

Books by Ann Roth

HARLEQUIN AMERICAN ROMANCE

1031—THE LAST TIME WE KISSED
1103—THE BABY INHERITANCE

Chapter One

Cinnamon Smith slowed her rented sedan to a crawl and peered through the windshield. The beam of her headlights cut through the darkness and the misty rain to illuminate a weathered sign. *Oceanside Bed and Breakfast*, it proclaimed in cheerfully scripted letters.

After listening for five years to Fran rave about the bed and breakfast she'd inherited, Cinnamon was finally here. Sighing with relief—she'd been on the road a good four hours since flying into Portland from L.A.—she pulled into the gravel driveway.

The past few weeks had been hellish, and she could hardly wait to relax and unwind. As she steered down the drive, floodlights blinked on, bathing the gray, shingled house in bright light. She braked to a stop in the large guest parking area beside the garage. Aside from a battered red pickup and Fran's SUV, hers was the only car.

Small wonder. Late January wasn't exactly tourist

season on the Oregon coast. The truck, she assumed, belonged to the man who Fran told her did odd jobs around the place.

As the inn's only guest, Cinnamon looked forward to cozy evenings with her closest friend and several much-needed heart-to-hearts. Fran always had been a down-to-earth, sensible person, and Cinnamon needed her calming influence. All two weeks of it. Actually, thirteen days—but close enough.

Mist tickled her face as she exited the car and stretched for the first time in hours. Slinging the strap of her purse over her shoulder, she squinted past the bright circle of light for a glimpse of the ocean. It was too dark to see anything, but Cinnamon smelled the sea's salty tang and heard the gentle slap of the waves. She could hardly wait to walk the beach.

Her hope was that the change of scenery would help put the past behind her, so she could move on and find a new job. Because the truth was, without her work as a business consultant, Cinnamon felt aimless, unimportant and scared. Her last day at Sabin and Howe had been Friday. She'd been unemployed three days now…. And with only three months' salary in savings, the familiar panicky feeling—racing heart, nausea and knots in her shoulders and neck—threatened to overwhelm her.

She forced a calming breath. There were plenty of companies in the world as good or better than Sabin and Howe. Hadn't she recently sent out e-mails to friends and colleagues in big consulting firms all over the country? Any day now she would surely hear back.

The thought filled her with hope, so much so that her stomach growled from hunger, a welcome change from weeks of no appetite. She retrieved her laptop and toiletries case from the trunk of the car, then swung those straps, too, onto her shoulder. Only the jumbo-size suitcase remained. Leaning into the trunk, she grabbed the handle and tugged. Filled with a parka, clothing, shoes and a pile of novels she meant to read, it weighed a good forty pounds, and she grunted with effort.

"I'll get that."

The large male at her side startled her. She hadn't heard him approach.

Gently nudging her over, he reached for the suitcase, his big, warm hand closing over her cold fist. Taken aback and not about to relinquish her bag, she tightened her grip and shot him the intimidating look that had cowed subordinates and peers alike. Until she'd been forced to resign from her job.

"Who are you?" Her breath made a cloud in the cold, damp air.

He pulled back and stepped aside. "Nick Mahoney. I work for Fran. I was on my way to the truck—" he gestured toward the red pickup "—to head home, and thought you could use a hand."

Thanks to the floodlights she noted his striking

blue eyes. His straight nose, strong chin and generous mouth were at the top of the handsome scale, too.

"Oh," she said. "Fran talks about you all the time. Sorry I was rude."

His gaze flickered over her, calf-length leather coat and all. Though still half bent over the suitcase, she sucked in her stomach.

The corner of his mouth lifted, charming her.

"Apology accepted."

"I...I'm Cinnamon Smith," she managed, suddenly wishing she'd combed her hair and freshened her makeup. She thought about shaking his hand, but decided against it and kept her fingers wrapped firmly around the handle of her suitcase.

"I know who you are. Fran's been yakking about your visit since last Friday."

"She has? Exactly what did she say?" Cinnamon trusted her friend not to reveal the details of her messy life, but the words had just tumbled out.

"That you two met in college and shared an apartment after, and that you haven't seen each other since she moved here and you became a hotshot executive. She's real excited about this visit." A roguish grin lit his face, as if he, too, looked forward to her being here.

Dear God, the man had a dimple in his cheek. Fran never had mentioned his looks. Was she blind?

"You going to let go of that bag, or would you rather carry it yourself?"

Her face felt hot and she knew she was blushing. "Um, you go ahead." She released the handle and straightened. "Thanks."

"My pleasure," he drawled.

Fran hadn't mentioned he was a flirt, either. Cinnamon was less than skilled at the art, and anyway, she was through with men. At least for a while. When she did decide to date again, she intended to find an upwardly mobile, career-focused, marriage-minded male, this time, single. Not some handyman, no matter how attractive he was. She pretended not to notice Nick's bold study of her.

He extracted the heavy suitcase as if it were as light as a sea breeze, then nodded toward the bed and breakfast. "The front door's up the steps on the ocean side of the house."

He strode forward. Cinnamon trailed him around the side of the building, then up the dozen wide wooden steps. Seemingly heedless of the winter chill, he wore no coat over his dark, long-sleeved T-shirt and snug, faded jeans. He was a big man with big limbs. Not heavy, but muscled and solid.

Despite being in excellent physical condition— she jogged three days a week—Cinnamon was slightly breathless, and not from the climb. Mentally she rolled her eyes.

She was here to pull herself together and, with the help of her laptop and the Internet, search out a new employer in a big city. She didn't need or want the distraction of any man.

Her gaze dropped to his rear end. My, oh, my…

Stop that, she silently scolded, frowning. It was no surprise that she lusted after the gorgeous male specimen before her. She hadn't had sex in over a month, since Dwight had dropped her because he'd reconciled with his wife—after repeatedly assuring Cinnamon that divorce was imminent and he wanted to marry her. The rat. His change of heart had left her with no option but to resign.

The familiar tension tightened her stomach. She willed it away. It was all in the past. Starting this very minute, she would forge ahead toward a new and better life.

With her chin raised in determination, Cinnamon followed Nick to the top of the steps.

CINNAMON GLANCED AT THE tiny white lights that lit up the Oceanside's wraparound, covered veranda. "This is charming."

"Wait till morning when you see that ocean view," Nick replied with a nod toward the darkness beyond.

The door was painted a warm, deep purple. The whimsical pelican-shaped metal knocker and the decorative heart wreath woven of sticks were so like Fran that Cinnamon smiled.

Nick wiped his feet on the thick, oval mat, also

purple, and opened the door. "Cinnamon's here," he called out, gesturing her inside.

The aromas of roast beef and baking bread filled the air, making her mouth water. Fran bustled into the room, thick braid swishing over her shoulder just as it had five years ago. Shoeless, she wore a beige *I Heart Cranberry, Oregon,* bib apron over a fuchsia-colored jumper and yellow turtleneck with matching yellow tights. Her love of vivid colors hadn't changed, either.

Even without shoes she stood a few inches taller than Cinnamon, who was exactly five-six —five-eight in the heeled boots she now wore.

"Hey, you," Fran said.

Wearing the grin Cinnamon knew and loved, eyes sparkling, Fran wiped her hands on the apron, then held out her arms.

It seemed ages since anyone had welcomed, let alone hugged, Cinnamon. Her eyes filled and she returned the embrace with equal warmth.

No crying, she sternly commanded herself. Crying was for pity parties, and hers was over. "It's so good to see you," she said, the words muffled in the hug. "Thanks for inviting me. I know you must be busy getting ready for the I Love the Oregon Coast Valentine Weekend and the tourist season after that."

Fran pulled back, smiling, to study her. "I *am* busy, but we'll have our evenings together. You've always been independent and resourceful, and I know you'll find plenty to occupy your time. I'm just so glad you're here, because talking on the phone several times a week isn't enough." She sobered. "How're you doing, hon?"

Cinnamon glanced at Nick. She knew he hadn't missed the concern in Fran's voice or her troubled expression. No doubt he was curious. She had plenty to discuss with her friend, but not now. "I'm managing," she said.

Fran nodded, then angled her head at Nick. "Thanks for carrying in that bag. You two introduced yourselves, I assume?"

"We sure did." His voice was teasing and ripe with innuendo.

He showered Cinnamon with a long, slow look that made her forget about her troubles. Her gaze flitted from his unnerving bedroom eyes to his chin, where a long, pale scar ran along his jaw, only noticeable in the bright light of the entry. Somehow that added to his attractiveness. Not that she was attracted. She was merely observing.

Liar.

She untied the belt of her leather coat and shrugged out of it. Or started to.

Nick set down her suitcase and helped, the perfect gentleman except for the warmer-than-warm gleam in his eyes and that seductive grin.

She felt herself blush. Again. Which only widened his smile. Clearly he knew his effect on women. Not so different from Dwight.

She frowned at him, but he had already turned away to hang up her coat.

"I'll take your bags to the room and then I'm off," he announced, grabbing the suitcase, laptop and cosmetic bag. He glanced at Fran. "The Orca suite?"

"Right."

"That's on the third floor," Cinnamon recalled. A veteran planner, before arriving she'd studied the layout of the Oceanside, using pictures from the Web site and the brochure Fran had mailed her. "The Oceanside's only suite. Luxurious, the brochure said."

"You'd better believe it," Nick commented. "Private bath with a whirlpool tub big enough for two." He raised his brows suggestively. "Sitting room, fireplace and a balcony overlooking the ocean. Takes up the whole floor." He winked. "You really rate." Whistling softly he headed up the carpeted staircase.

When he was out of sight, Fran leaned toward her. "Isn't he adorable?" she whispered.

"I was thinking more along the lines of hot and sexy." Cinnamon shot her friend a reproachful smirk. "You never mentioned his looks."

"Oops. Guess I forgot."

"Well, he's not my type. Right now, no man is." Bruised feelings, dangerously close to the surface, threatened to spill out in a hot rush of tears. *Not now, not now.*

Cinnamon glanced around the brightly lit foyer and beyond to the blazing fire in the other room. "That's the great room you rent out for weddings and parties. As I recall from the brochure, 'The main level's open floor plan allows guests easy access between the great room, dining room and kitchen.' I can't wait to see everything."

Amusement twinkled in Fran's eyes. "You memorized that?"

"Not really." Cinnamon shrugged. "I read the brochure carefully, several times. That's known as attention to detail."

"Attention to detail, eh?" Her friend outright laughed. "That is so like you. And the reason you're such a good consultant."

"*Used* to be good, you mean."

The humor faded from Fran's expression. "You're still the best, hon. We all make mistakes." There was no judgment or condemnation in the words or in her face, only compassion and love. "Ease up on yourself."

Fresh tears filled Cinnamon's eyes. Jeez, she was sensitive tonight. She blinked furiously. "Can we please talk about something else?"

"Sure." Fran patted her arm, offering reassurance. "How about a quick tour after Nick leaves?"

They both heard the thud of his footsteps on the carpeted stairs and his tuneless whistle.

"Speak of the devil," Fran quipped.

Grinning, Nick glanced from one woman to the other. "You two talking about me?"

His confident stance and lowered eyelids showed Cinnamon he assumed he was the topic of conversation. "You wish," she said, letting her irritation show.

"Ouch." Laying his hand over his heart he gave her a mock-wounded frown that lightened her mood a fraction.

"I'm sure you'll live," Fran said. "Thanks for taking the bags up, and thanks for your hard work today. See you tomorrow?"

"You bet." He saluted, fingers flirting with his overlong hair. "Right after I drop Abby at school."

So he had a daughter. Probably a wife, too, though Fran hadn't mentioned that. Yet here he was, flirting and looking at Cinnamon with I-want-you lust. Men! She shot him a you-cad frown, but he was focused on Fran.

"I have a dentist appointment first thing in the morning, and a long city council meeting after that, so I may not be around," Fran said. "Cinnamon will let you in."

One eyebrow quirked up. "I'll look for-ward to that. You ladies have fun tonight. Don't do anything I wouldn't do, but if you do," he aimed yet another suggestive look at Cinnamon, "think of me."

He was cocky and trite and married. She could

hardly stand him, yet at the same time, the attention felt wonderful. How pathetic was that?

Moisture gathered behind her eyes. *Don't cry. Don't!* Her tears were too near the surface to risk speaking. She swallowed them back.

In a blink Nick's expression turned solemn and wary, as if he understood she was an emotional wreck. Well, she never had been good at hiding her feelings.

"What'd I do?" he asked, his soft, contrite tone totally devoid of flirtation.

"It's not you," she said in a voice clogged with emotion.

The sympathy and kindness in his eyes snapped her shaky control. She burst into tears.

FEELING HELPLESS AND UNCOMFORTABLE, Nick shifted from one foot to the other. He thought Cinnamon was cute in an uptight, corporate sort of way, and he'd enjoyed teasing her and making her cheeks flame. She was way out of his league, but not immune to his attention. But then, flirting was one thing he knew he was good at.

Now the teasing was forgotten. Crying females scared him. They always had. Even his sister and niece. Abby took shameless advantage of the knowledge, too, and she was only twelve.

But Cinnamon wasn't trying to wheedle something out of him. Her bawling was genuine. His chest felt tight. He wished he could help, but the woman had plenty of smarts and an advanced degree in business, while he'd barely squeaked through high school, graduating at twenty. A guy like him had nothing to offer her.

And no business watching her fall apart. He looked longingly at the door, but unfortunately his escape was blocked by Fran and her sobbing friend.

"It'll all be okay, hon," she soothed, her arm around Cinnamon. "C'mon, let's go into the great room and sit down."

Cinnamon ducked under her grasp and visibly pulled herself together. Attention fixed on the oak floor, she swiped at her eyes and sniffled. "I…I'm fine now."

So she said. But tears continued to stream down her cheeks. She wasn't through crying yet.

Fran caught his eye. "There's a box of tissues in the powder room."

Nick nodded. On his way to the bathroom he passed the large, sliding-glass door along the wall of the dining room, which opened onto the veranda. Beyond that were the kitchen and the basement stairs, leading to the garage with its door to the side yard.

He thought about sneaking out either exit, but Cinnamon needed those tissues. So he retrieved the box and returned to the great room, where a cozy fire crackled in the massive stone fireplace.

The two women sat side by side on the long sofa, their backs to him. He saw their reflection in the floor-to-ceiling ocean-view windows across the room, backlit by the tiny lights on the veranda.

Cinnamon's bowed head rested in her hands, her short, dark, spiky hair sticking up between her fingers. She wasn't crying anymore, though. Wasn't talking, either. It was Fran's voice he heard, though she spoke so softly he couldn't make out the words.

He wondered what had happened to cause Cinnamon to break down in front of him. Whatever it was, he wanted no part of it. He'd hand over the tissues and leave. As Nick trudged reluctantly into the room the oven timer buzzed.

"That's the bread." Fran jumped up. "Excuse me." With a worried look Cinnamon didn't see, she glanced at Nick and jerked her head toward Cinnamon.

No way could he leave, now.

Sniffling, Cinnamon reached for the tissue box. "Thanks," she said, blowing her nose.

With a stiff nod he backed toward the pair of armchairs catty-corner to the sofa. He didn't sit, though, because he wouldn't be here long enough for that.

Her red, swollen eyes met his, then skittered away, but he saw the bleak expression there. With the dark smudges of makeup on her cheeks she sure didn't look like an executive anymore. Not so pretty, either.

Then why did he suddenly want to kiss her? He

imagined cupping her face between his hands, lowering his head and teasing her lips until the shadows vanished from her eyes. Then he'd deepen the kiss and— *Get real, fool.*

Frowning, he stuffed his hands into his back pockets and cleared his throat. "You done crying?"

She nodded and tried to smile but didn't quite make it. "I don't know what came over me. I've had a rough few weeks, and I guess they finally caught up with me."

The way she was looking up at him, he figured she expected him to say something. He shrugged. "I've had a few of those myself along the way."

"I'll bet you didn't cry, though, did you?"

Inside he had—every time some kid called him a stupid moron. "Men aren't supposed to."

"Corporate vice presidents aren't, either. Of course, now that I'm an ex-corporate vice president…" She laughed, a dry noise that sounded as if it hurt.

So she'd lost her high-level job. Given all those tears, that must have stung badly. He searched his mind for the right thing to say. "A woman like you should be able to find a new job fast."

She pulled in a shuddering breath, and for a moment he feared she'd cry again. To his relief she sat up straight and squared her shoulders. This time she looked squarely at him.

"Thank you for the vote of confidence."

Holding her head high allowed him a nice view of her long, slender neck. He'd always liked necks, and hers was about perfect. Was it as smooth as it looked? He would never know, and he had no business thinking that way. What in hell was wrong with him?

"Need anything else?" he asked, eyeing her guardedly.

She shook her head.

"Then I'll be leaving."

He got out of there as fast as he could.

Chapter Two

Appalled at her temporary lapse of self-control—blubbering like a weak fool in front of a man she barely knew!—Cinnamon cringed on the sofa until the click of the front door signaled Nick's departure.

In her mind she saw his uncomfortable expression. He was so eager to get away from her he'd practically sprinted to the door. She released a groan of humiliation, and buried her face in her hands.

But rehashing and getting stressed over what had just happened would only make her feel worse. It would be better for her to occupy her mind another way—perhaps a to-do list for the rest of the evening and tomorrow. But for that she needed her Palm Pilot, which, unfortunately, was in the laptop bag Nick had taken up-stairs. Since she felt emotionally exhausted and not ready to move, she settled for composing the list in her head, imagining little bullet points arranged in chronological order.

First, find the kitchen and assure Fran that she was okay, because darn it, she was. Then head upstairs to the suite to wash her face and comb her hair. After dinner a tour of the Oceanside and—

"The bread is cooling, the potatoes are simmering and the roast is nearly done," Fran announced.

Cinnamon jerked in surprise. Deep in concentration, she hadn't heard her friend come into the room.

"Great."

Frowning, Fran glanced around. "Did Nick leave?"

"A few minutes ago. I was about to come find you." Scooping the handful of used tissues from her lap, Cinnamon stood.

"Toss those in the fireplace," Fran advised. She aimed a concerned gaze at Cinnamon. "Are you feeling better now?"

Her unwelcome outburst was the last thing Cinnamon wanted to discuss, but knowing Fran, she'd push and prod until Cinnamon answered the question. As she wandered to the fireplace she let out a sigh. "I'm drained and totally embarrassed, but yes, definitely better."

Fran nodded. "I suspect you needed a good cry, and if you can't do that with your best friend…" She shrugged. "What I'm saying is, don't waste your energy feeling embarrassed."

"Nick isn't my best friend. I just met the man, and he saw me at my worst." Face hot both from the heat of the fire and humiliation, Cinnamon lobbed the used tissues into the flames. Hissing, the yellow tendrils flared up, obliterating all traces of paper. If only she could wipe out her problems so easily.

"What he saw was a woman hurting—nothing to be ashamed of," Fran said. "Anyway, it's over now. How about a quick tour before dinner, ending at your room? I'm sure you want to freshen up." She pulled a screen in front of the hearth.

Grateful for the new subject, Cinnamon managed a smile. "Sounds good."

"We'll start right here, in the great room." Fran waved her hand toward the huge area, which, aside from the big, comfortable furniture, was mostly floor-to-ceiling glass and open space.

"It's beautiful, perfect for parties," Cinnamon commented. She wandered to the chest-high bookcase separating the great and dining rooms, crammed with paperback books. "If I'd known about these, I wouldn't have brought my own stash. I can't wait to see the rest of the place."

Fran nodded. "My apartment is in the basement, which I'll show you later. If you need to do laundry, the washer and dryer are down there, too. Let's start with this floor. This way to the dining room." She beckoned Cinnamon past the bookcase. "Even though I could eat in the kitchen and sometimes do—" she glanced at the adjacent room "—I like to take my meals here, because of the ocean view. Wait till tomorrow morning and you'll understand." Pausing a moment she frowned at the floor-to-ceiling windows and sliding glass doors. "Though, the windows need a good washing. Remind me to ask Nick about that."

The little white lights on the veranda seemed to wink at Cinnamon. Nick had winked at her, too. She frowned. "He's a big flirt."

Her friend, who was headed for the pearl-colored counter that separated the dining room from the kitchen, stopped and pivoted toward her. "Nothing wrong with a little harmless flirtation," she said, shifting the loaf of bread that was cooling on the counter. "As I recall, you didn't mind."

"I can't believe what I'm hearing," Cinnamon scoffed. "The man is married with a daughter. He shouldn't be flirting."

"Married?" Fran's jaw dropped. "Where in the world did you get an idea like that?" She rounded the counter and headed into the kitchen, Cinnamon following.

"When he mentioned his daughter. May I have a glass of water?"

Fran opened a pearl-colored cabinet door, which seemed to glow in contrast to the apricot-colored walls. "Help yourself. Abby is his niece," she continued as Cinnamon took a glass. "Her mom, a single mother and Nick's older sister, starts work at the cran-

berry factory, which I suggest you tour, at seven-thirty.
She drops Abby at Nick's and he drives her to school.
FYI, at the moment he's between girlfriends—single
and definitely available."

"Oh." Cinnamon didn't understand her relief at the
news. She wandered to the sink. The window above
it faced the same direction as the dining and great
rooms. "After Dwight, I guess I'm paranoid."

"Not all men are like that snake."

"You mean pursuing a subordinate—that would be
me—while separated from his wife, convincing said
subordinate that once the divorce came through, *she*
was what he wanted, starting a sexual relationship,
and then changing his mind and going back to his
wife? Which forced the subordinate to resign? Gee, I
hope not." No tears now. She was too angry at Dwight
and her own foolish self to cry.

"You'll get past this."

"I know." She sounded a lot more convincing than
she felt.

Fran bustled to the stove and peered into a simmering pot. Then she turned her attention to Cinnamon.
"Did you really love him?"

For a moment Cinnamon considered the question.
"I thought I did. Otherwise I never would have slept
with him."

Fran gave her a curious look she couldn't ignore.
Knowing she was about to reveal an unflattering side

of herself, Cinnamon bit her lip. "Dwight Sabin is successful, sophisticated, well read and fun to be with— all things I want in a husband. And I am so ready to get married. So when he left his wife and then pursued *me*... I was more than flattered." And utterly foolish. She paused for a sip of water. "I never realized how other people saw our relationship until it was too late."

The snide looks and comments, some from supposed friends, had stung. Babette Cousins, another vice president, had called her a "scheming bitch determined to sleep her way up the corporate ladder." Untrue, and so hurtful!

"Boy, was I dumb." Cinnamon managed a laugh, flat and humorless as it was. "If I ever again mention dating a man separated from his wife, will you just shoot me?"

"I think you've learned your lesson." Fran opened the lower of her two ovens, nodded to herself and turned it off. "And I truly believe you're on the mend. That spicy undercurrent between you and Nick? I could actually feel the sparks—before you burst into tears."

"Don't remind me." Mortification scalded Cinnamon's cheeks as she knocked her fist against her forehead. "I'm not interested in Nick. When I decide to date again, the man I choose will be ambitious and earn a big salary."

"That's your choice, of course."

The slight edge to Fran's tone puzzled Cinnamon. She frowned. "What's that supposed mean?"

"Let me answer that with a question. Counting Dwight, how many men have you been involved with over the past five years?"

"In actual relationships? Three."

Fran nodded. "All corporate climbers and all slime-balls. I see a definite pattern here, and I suggest you rethink the kind of man you want. There's more to life than ambition and money."

"You wouldn't say that if you'd grown up poor."

Cinnamon had. Her mother didn't like to work, and flitted from job to job. They'd lived hand to mouth, often moving in the dead of night to avoid paying the rent.

"But you earn more than enough to live the good life," Fran pointed out. "You don't need a male to depend on."

"True, but I want someone with the same ambitions and goals as me, a man who understands the importance of balancing a successful career with family. Anyway, for now I'm taking a break from men."

"That seems sensible." Fran gestured beyond the kitchen. "If we want to finish our tour before dinner, we'd best get on with it."

As Nick drove toward Cranberry Grade and High School, his usually talkative niece was quiet, her head bent over a math book. Serious and a perfectionist by nature, this morning she radiated tension.

A kid shouldn't be so uptight. He decided to lighten up her mood. Rounding a bend in the tree-lined, winding road he gestured out the window. "Just look at that sky. Not a single cloud. If I didn't know better I'd think spring was around the corner instead of months away."

"Uh-huh," Abby replied without raising her head from the book.

Braking at a four-way stop, he frowned his disapproval and waited for the compact in front of them to go. "Don't you think you studied enough?"

She flipped her shoulder-length hair behind her ear, and Nick caught her worried look. "In case you forgot, the practice math bee is today."

"How could I, when that's all you talk about? It's only a warm-up, kid, so relax."

"I'm fine," she insisted, tightening her lips in the familiar way that reminded Nick of her mom.

Nick snorted. "The heck you are." The compact turned, and he headed forward. "You're so tense, you're about to snap. I can't imagine what you'll be like before the real math bee." Which was Friday morning, in Portland.

"Don't you get it? Even if this is a practice, I have to be the best." Her small brow furrowed. "If I don't win, I won't get invited to the math camp in Virginia this summer. So puh-leeze let me study." Her attention returned to her book.

"Suit yourself." They drove the rest of the way in silence.

His niece had been jabbering since third grade about the exclusive camp, a program designed for kids twelve through eighteen. Each age group competed for math bee state champion, and only the winners were allowed in.

Abby really wanted to go, and Nick figured she stood a strong chance. But winning a coveted invitation wasn't enough. The two-week program cost a bundle. A special math grant paid for the tuition, but room, board and airfare were the responsibility of the family—in this case, Nick, since Sharon couldn't pay. Not with her bills. As it was she barely scraped by. And with the cranberry factory up for sale and rumors of possible layoffs or worse...

He stopped himself. He wouldn't think about that, not with Abby in the car. Both he and Sharon had agreed there was no sense adding that worry to the kid's already burdened little shoulders.

He glanced at his niece, whose lips moved as she whispered to herself. She deserved to go to the camp with other kids like her. Who knew what could come out of that? Maybe a scholarship to college. Nick didn't have the smarts to go that route, but Abby did. She'd be the first person in the Mahoney family to attend and graduate from college.

Then, who knew? She might end up vice president

of some corporation. Like Cinnamon. Except she'd lost her job.

Beyond the trees lining the ocean side of the street, morning sunlight dappled the water. Squinting, he reached for the sunglasses above the visor. He'd thought about Cinnamon way more than he wanted, first on the drive home last night and later while lying in bed. After working hard clearing dead brush from around Fran's foundation yesterday he should have fallen asleep as soon as his head hit the pillow.

But no, he'd spent a frustrating few hours fantasizing about *her*. Massaging the strain from her beautiful nape while she poured out her troubles. He would nuzzle the sensitive place where her neck and shoulder met, making her groan with pleasure. She would angle her face just so, silently begging him to kiss her. First he'd taste the tears. Then, when her lips parted and her breathing shallowed, he'd take her mouth in a deep, hot kiss.

His body stirred to life and his hands stroked the steering wheel the same as he wanted to stroke and arouse her body. Pretty soon she'd forget all about crying and losing her job...

As if she'd ever want you.

Nick scowled, but that was the truth. The females he dated didn't have advanced degrees. They laughed often and partied hard. They wanted what he wanted—good times and satisfying sex. Which wasn't always enough…and one reason why he never stayed with the same woman for long. But it worked for him.

Cinnamon was smart, educated and classy, a woman as far out of his reach as the moon. Unless he wanted trouble and a bucket of pain, he'd best remember that.

"We're almost at school," he said, waiting for Abby to get her nose out of the math book. "Now, I want you to listen to your uncle Nick."

She let out a sigh far too world weary for a twelve-year-old. "What?"

"You're going to ace the practice math bee *and* win the real thing," he stated as he turned onto Gray Whale Street, where the school was. "I know it—" he thumped his chest "—in here."

Abby rolled her eyes. "You only feel that way 'cause I'm your niece."

He shook his head. "No, I feel that way because you're the smartest kid in sixth grade, and the brainiest math whiz in the whole school. Just remember to relax. Your mind can't work right if you're too tense."

He knew this from personal experience. Give him time to puzzle out the words on a page and he could. Hurry him along and make him uptight, and the print looked as foreign as Arabic.

"How do I relax?" she asked, her forehead puckered.

"Simple. Just take a deep breath." He drew in a

breath and watched her do the same. "Now blow it out." They both did. "Tell yourself, 'I can handle this.' Then trust your brain and let it do its thing."

"Hey, that's pretty cool." His niece looked at him thoughtfully. "Where did you learn it?"

"From Mr. Edison, a high school teacher of mine."

The man who at last had diagnosed Nick's learning problems as dyslexia, not mental retardation. At the time, Nick had been sixteen, still stuck in ninth grade and about to drop out. Mr. Edison had persuaded him to work hard and graduate. Four years later he had. His mother had died shortly after that, and he'd left town and moved to Cranberry to start a new life.

Abby knew nothing about his reading problem. Nobody in Cranberry did except Sharon, who had followed him here eleven years ago. She'd promised to keep his secret, and so far had kept her word. In all those years she'd never brought up the subject. Neither had he, which was how he wanted things.

He shrugged at his niece. "What do you think? Gonna try it today?"

Her taut expression easing, she nodded. "Thanks, Uncle Nick."

When she closed her book and slipped it into her backpack, Nick gave a mental sigh of relief. Mission accomplished.

"How about I take you and your mom to Rosy's

tonight to celebrate?" The diner was a family favorite, and easy on the wallet.

"You mean if I win?"

"You will," he said. "But even if you don't, you deserve a celebration for working so hard. And to keep up your strength for the real math bee." Signaling, he followed a school bus into the drop-off area. "Wish I could be there today to support you, but with the Valentine holiday coming up, Fran needs me."

The actual tourist season started at the beginning of April, but the days around February 14 drew plenty of couples who were eager for a romantic getaway. After that the tourist trade built and grew until the town hummed with visitors.

Nick was glad of the work. He liked Fran and she paid well. True, he would prefer Cinnamon not be there, but if he stuck to a brief "hi" and focused on work, he'd be way too busy to think about her. He hoped. Since he needed to stop at the lumberyard this morning, he might not even see her today. That'd help.

In any case, she was only here two weeks. In that short amount of time he could put up with anything, even misplaced sexual desire.

"That's okay, Uncle Nick, because we need the money. As long as you come with Mom and me to Portland."

"Wouldn't miss that for the world," he vowed as he turned right. Even if it did mean leaving Thursday and driving four hours to get there, and precious money spent on a motel. Necessary tolls on Abby's road to success.

He braked to a stop at the drop-off area. School kids of all ages skipped and strolled toward the building's entrance.

"Have fun at Fran's, and tell her 'hi' from me." Abby opened the passenger door.

A year ago he would have tousled her hair, but she didn't like that anymore. She was growing up way too fast.

He settled for a thumb's-up. "'Bye, kid. Don't forget to breathe. Then knock 'em dead."

Her shoulders squared. "I will."

SHOWERED AND DRESSED, Palm Pilot tucked reassuringly into the pocket of her cardigan, Cinnamon moved purposefully down the stairs. It was still dark outside, but she was used to waking up early for work. Besides, Fran was leaving for a dentist appointment shortly, and Cinnamon wanted to eat breakfast with her.

Speaking of breakfast… The fragrant aromas of fresh-brewed coffee, frying bacon and baking treats filled the air. Cinnamon hurried across the foyer, her mouth watering. Near the kitchen she heard her friend's voice. Who was she talking to?

Nick. Cinnamon faltered. She didn't want to face the

man, especially first thing this morning. She stopped outright. Maybe she'd sneak back to her room or take a beach walk, an activity she'd entered on her Palm Pilot to-do list, now instead of later. But Fran had prepared a meal, and Cinnamon wanted to enjoy it with her.

She frowned. What was she afraid of, anyway? At least today she'd applied makeup and fixed her hair, the very actions bolstering her self-esteem. Today she looked like her usual composed self and felt firmly in control of her emotions. She would simply pretend nothing had happened last night That was how she'd survived the last awful weeks at Sabin and Howe.

In quick order she smoothed the pullover turtleneck under her matching cardigan, fluffed her hair with her fingers and pasted a polite smile on her face. Ignoring the knot in her stomach, she strode confidently into the kitchen.

To her surprise she saw only Fran. "Good morning," she greeted, glancing around with bewilderment. "I swear, I heard you talking to someone."

"Hey, you." Dressed in a cheery red sweater and matching cords covered by a bright blue bib apron, Fran stood at the stove over a skillet of sizzling bacon. "What you heard was my side of a conversation with Stubby and Stumpy, my seagull friends. They're not much for chitchat, but they're great listeners." She glanced at the sliding glass doors in the dining room. "They were sitting in their usual place on the railing, but flew off when they saw you."

For years Cinnamon had heard about the gulls Fran had "adopted," both with permanent injuries. She followed her friend's gaze, her attention stretching beyond the veranda. The view, matched only by the view from her suite, was spectacular—about twenty yards of sandy beach and an unobstructed vista of ocean beneath a clear blue sky.

"What an incredible view," she breathed.

"Didn't I tell you? This time of year we rarely get sunny days, so be sure you take advantage of the nice weather and get out on the beach."

"That's on my list." Cinnamon patted her pocket, feeling the Palm Pilot. "I hope the gulls come back, so I can meet them."

"Don't worry, they haven't eaten yet. They'll hang around until I feed them. Today is Wednesday, which means bacon. Extra crisp, or they throw fits. And the cheese-and-mushroom frittata had better be warm."

Cinnamon laughed. "Sounds as if they have you wrapped around their little feet."

Amusement sparkled in Fran's eyes, and a grin lit her face. "You're so right."

Badly in need of coffee, Cinnamon opened a cabinet stocked with cups, saucers and mugs. "I thought you were talking to Nick."

That earned her a shrewd look. "You should see the expression on your face. I don't care what you said last night. You're interested in him."

"And you're dead wrong." Cinnamon chose a large, red mug emblazoned with two gulls soaring over the Oceanside Bed and Breakfast sign. "I meant what I said. I'm through with men, at least for now. The truth is, I'd rather avoid Nick."

"You're still wasting energy on what happened last night?"

When Cinnamon sheepishly nodded, Fran tsked. "Nick's good people, and I'm sure he's forgotten the whole thing. Besides, by the time he shows up, you may be out. He called a few minutes ago to let me know he was at the lumberyard outside town, picking up a few things. Could be a while before he arrives. He'll be working on the veranda today, replacing some rotted floorboards, but he needs access to the house, for the bathroom and so forth. So leave the sliding door unlocked."

"Will do." Cinnamon didn't understand the sharp prick of disappointment that followed Fran's announcement. She wanted to steer clear of Nick, yet at the same time hoped to see him.

Which was thoroughly mystifying and not at all the way she ought to feel. Pushing aside her confusion, she filled her mug. Regardless, she wouldn't be facing him today.

"NEED HELP COOKING?" Cinnamon asked as Fran bustled around the kitchen. She wasn't used to being waited on. Even as a child, she'd been the one cooking breakfast for herself and her mother, who would have been content with coffee and cigarettes.

Fran shook her head. "This is part of what I do for my guests."

"But I'm not really a guest. I'm your best friend."

"You insist on paying for your room, so you're both."

"Yes, but you gave me a cheap rate. Way too low for a luxurious suite."

Fran waved off the words. "I gave you the off-season rate. So you like the suite?"

"Who wouldn't love plush carpeting, a king-size bed covered with soft, flannel sheets and a fat down comforter? Or the cozy sitting room with fireplace, *and* the private balcony overlooking the ocean? Yours is as lovely as a suite at any four-star hotel," Cinnamon gushed. "This whole place is fabulous. I'm no small-town girl, but if I had an aunt Franny like you did, and she left me this place… You're one lucky woman."

"Don't I know it. Even if you do prefer the hustle and bustle of big cities, you'll like Cranberry. I wish I could spend all day showing you around, but with the Valentine's Day festivities almost upon us and me on the activities-planning committee, and the meetings with the town council to keep them informed…" Fran shook her head. "Lately I'm so darn busy, it's not even funny."

"I could use some of that." Cinnamon stifled a pang of envy. "Don't worry about me. I have plenty to keep me busy." She'd typed a to-do list into her Palm Pilot to prove it.

"What do you mean, 'busy'?" Fran shot her a sharp look. "I thought you were here to relax."

Cinnamon didn't really know how to do that, but she intended to try. "I will, I promise. But I need a new job and I want to start looking. I sent out e-mails to colleagues in New York, San Francisco and Minneapolis," she added, "and I want to follow up on their replies."

"But this is supposed to be a vacation." The scolding tone was softened by Fran's concerned expression. "You haven't had one in years. Give yourself time away from the work world. You've earned that."

True enough. For the past five years Cinnamon had been too wrapped up in work to take off more than a few days here and there. But she enjoyed working because it gave her life purpose. Also, she hadn't saved as much as she should, and draining her savings was going to hurt.

"I can't enjoy myself with unemployment hanging over my head," she said. "But I do plan to spend a good chunk of time taking in the sights and getting to know the area. I thought I'd tour the cranberry factory this afternoon, after I walk the beach."

"I'm glad to hear that." Fran looked relieved. "Now take your coffee into the dining room and let me finish this bacon. Oh, and help yourself to the cranberry juice. There's a pitcher on the table."

"No OJ?" Cinnamon made a face.

"If you want. But this *is* Cranberry, Oregon, and since our cranberry factory employs ten percent of the population, the chamber of commerce has asked all restaurants, motels and bed-and-breakfasts to serve the juice every morning." Fran looked solemn. "Though to tell you the truth, the factory isn't doing well. It's been for sale for over a year with no takers. Now there are rumors that soon people will be laid off. The business may even close its doors for good. We'll be discussing the situation at this afternoon's town council meeting." She gave her head a dismal shake. "That won't be pleasant."

As a management consultant, Cinnamon earned her living working with companies struggling to survive. Sounded as if this one could be on its last legs. "Sorry to hear that," she said. "I'll definitely drink cranberry juice this morning."

She wandered into the dining room. With the table positioned in front of the sliding glass door, every seat commanded a view of the ocean. As soon as she settled into a chair, two scrappy seagulls, no doubt the pair Fran had adopted and spoiled, lit on the deck's wooden railing directly in her line of vision.

"Nice to meet you at last," she said, tipping her mug their direction.

Standing side by side, they watched her with cocked heads. Their beaks opened and closed as if they expected her to toss them treats. Through the window she heard their pleading shrieks.

"Begging, are you? Unless you drink coffee or cranberry juice, you're out of luck," she told them.

From the kitchen, Fran laughed. "Oh, they'll get theirs."

As the birds blinked and hop-stepped like a pair of vaudeville comedians, Cinnamon couldn't help chuckling, too. "They sure are entertaining. Which is which?"

Leaning across the counter that divided the kitchen and dining room, Fran peered at the beggars. "Stumpy's the one with no webbing on his foot. Stubs is holding up his left leg." She walked into the room with a half-dozen steaming blueberry muffins arranged in an attractive metal basket, then set it and a platter of still-sizzling bacon on the table.

The timer on the top oven buzzed. "There's the frittata," Fran said.

Seconds later she brought the egg dish into the dining room, setting off a frenzy outside. Both gulls flapped their wings and opened their beaks, making loud, demanding squawks.

"Patience, boys," Fran said. "You'll eat after we finish." She shook out her napkin and placed it on her lap.

"We'd better eat fast," Cinnamon said. "No telling what they'll do if we take too long."

"They'll wait. *Bon appetit.*"

For several long moments they ate in amiable silence, enjoying the food. Far too soon Fran glanced at her watch.

"If I want to make that dentist appointment on time, I'd better feed the birds and scoot. I'll be back late this afternoon. I thought we'd eat at Rosy's Diner tonight, one of my favorite restaurants. The fridge is full of cold cuts, so if you're here during lunch, help yourself. Oh, and there's a spare house key hanging on the hook by the back door. Be sure to take it with you when you go out, in case Nick leaves before you get back and locks the sliders."

"I'll clean up the kitchen," Cinnamon volunteered.

"Everything goes in the dishwasher." Fran piled the gulls' breakfast onto old Melmac plates, which she set on the veranda. Car keys in hand, she waved as she headed down the basement steps. "'Bye, hon."

A moment later the garage door squeaked open, squeaking again as it closed. Cinnamon waited for the gulls to devour their meal, then collected their empty plates and brought them inside. In no time she straightened up the kitchen. She phoned the cranberry factory and set up an afternoon tour, then returned to the dining room to enjoy a leisurely second cup of coffee, a luxury she wasn't used to. Nice as it should be to sit awhile, doing nothing made her antsy. For years she'd rushed off to work at the crack of dawn. Now she was free and easy. And alone.

The gulls, who had flown off a moment ago, returned to study her. She watched them with delight and tried to relax. Instead she felt unsettled and at loose ends. Lost. Unemployed, no better than her mother.

A disturbing thought. Panic tightened her chest, and her stomach twinged uncomfortably. "I'm not like her," she sternly admonished. "I want to work."

She decided to spend some time online this morning and call a few colleagues.

Mollified, she stared at the whitecaps dancing in the ocean. But the fluttery movement, or maybe the second cup of coffee, made her restless, and the worry crept back. *What if I can't find consulting work?*

"Then I'll do something else," she stated, sick and tired of herself. *Relax.* She slid her Palm Pilot from her pocket and clicked it on, the familiar activity anchoring her. Fran had left several brochures on the counter. Cinnamon decided to pore over those and figure out which places to visit during her stay here. Then she'd take that walk, which should help calm her nerves.

She spread the brochures on the table. Unlike the big cities she preferred, Cranberry offered no art museums or cultural events. But the whale watching looked interesting. Unfortunately the company was closed till April. The game park was open, though, and it looked promising, as did the historical museum. Hmm…

Loud squawks jerked her attention outside. Wings flapping, the gulls soared away. Footsteps thudded on the deck, and Cinnamon's stomach flip-flopped.

Nick had arrived.

Chapter Three

Huffing from exertion, breath visible in the chill air, Nick set a heavy blue tarp and circular saw on the veranda. Late January wasn't the best time of year to replace the deck's rotting floorboards, because of the cold. But with the Valentine's Day holiday in a few weeks, followed by a steadily growing parade of tourists that would last through late October, now was the best time.

He would need to make a good six trips across the veranda and up and down the steps for the rest of his supplies—a table for his circular saw he'd designed specially for this job, tools, nails, cedar tongue-and-groove planks and the sawhorse. Lugging all of that and a cup of hot coffee ought to warm him up.

Nick drank a lot of the stuff, and Fran kept a pot ready for him. Blowing warmth into his icy hands, he headed for the sliding doors off the dining room.

Damned if Cinnamon wasn't scrambling up from

the table. Nick hesitated. She'd been watching him and he hadn't even realized it. For some reason that both irritated and excited him. He frowned. Wasn't she supposed to be gone by now, sightseeing or whatever? No big deal. He'd stick to his plan—say hello, fill his mug and get to work.

His feet scraped the welcome mat, then he slid open the door. "Morning."

"Hi." Without quite meeting his eyes she offered a stiff nod and a flimsy smile.

Could she be any more tense? Nick remembered a similar forced expression on her face last night. He hoped to God she didn't start bawling.

"You feeling okay this morning?"

Relying on the flirtation that stood him well with women and put them at ease, he let his gaze slide over her. The fatigue had vanished from her face, and her eyes were clear. Without last night's unhappiness spoiling her features, she was more than pretty. Nice clothes, too. Her pale blue sweater set outlined her breasts, and navy slacks hinted at round hips and long, slender legs. He raised his eyebrows approvingly. "You sure look good."

The flush he liked rose to her cheeks. "I'm much better, thanks."

He saw no sign of tears. That was a relief.

"I don't usually break down like that," she went on, clutching a cell-phone-size gadget as if she needed to hold on to something. "I'd appreciate it if you forgot the whole thing."

"I'd forget my own name if that kept you from crying."

"I was that bad, huh?"

Her lips twitched, but he wanted a full grin. "I don't know," he teased, "since I can't remember what we're talking about."

Her mouth curved and widened as the smile he sought bloomed on her face. Beautiful. At last she looked straight at him.

"Me neither. Thanks."

Sunlight from the window lit up her eyes. They were an unusual rust brown. He hadn't noticed last night. "Is that how you got your name? From your cinnamon-color eyes?"

They widened in surprise, and she nodded. "Thea—that's my mother—couldn't decide what to name me. I was 'Baby Girl' until my eyes turned this color when I was around six months old."

"No kidding." Nick shook his head. "I've always been Nick, the same as my old man."

"I never knew my father," Cinnamon said. "According to Thea he could have been any of several."

Her fingers fidgeted with the gadget, and he knew she was uncomfortable again. He understood and didn't like sharing his personal life, either.

Yet he sought to reassure her by sharing a part

of his past. "I didn't have much of one, myself. My old man split when I was ten, and I haven't seen or heard from him since. Now Mom's gone, too. Bad heart."

"Sorry to hear that." Sympathy flashed across her face.

"Thanks."

He turned toward the kitchen, brushing past her. At least, that was the plan.

His arm grazed hers. Though they both wore long sleeves, the touch jolted him. She must have felt the strong current, too, for awareness darkened her eyes. He jerked away and started again for the kitchen.

"Did you want something?"

Oh, yeah, but nothing he cared to voice. He stopped and turned toward her, hooking his thumbs on his tool belt. "That depends…"

She glanced at his belt, then lower. Her gaze flew upward, as if she hadn't meant to look there. "In the kitchen, I mean," she added, slightly breathless.

"Just gettin' my coffee."

"Great. Fine." Clutching the gadget in both hands, she gave her head a vigorous nod.

Frowning, Nick eyed her. "Are you afraid of me?"

"Of course not." Now she clasped the gadget to her chest.

"What is that thing?" he asked.

"A Palm Pilot. I keep my whole life in it—address

book, appointments, goals and my daily to-do list. Everything."

She smoothed her fingers lovingly over the burgundy cover. One-track mind that he had, he wished he were that gadget.

"You have a to-do list while you're here?" He puzzled over that. "I thought you were on vacation."

"You sound just like Fran," she said, exasperation in her voice. "I'll tell you exactly what I told her. I *am* on vacation. As you know, I'm also unemployed." Her nose wrinkled in distaste. "I can't very well find a new job without looking for one, can I?"

"I guess not. But can't you remember that in your brain?"

Up went her head, queenlike. "Of course I can, but I have more than a few daily goals." She shot him a "doesn't everybody" look. "Why not let the Palm Pilot do my remembering for me? That way I can free up my mind for other things. Since I'm a planner by nature, every night before bed I make a list and rank-order it. In the morning I look it over, adding or changing the items—same as I've been doing for years."

"Years, huh." Nick kept his schedule in his head. She was way too organized and structured for him. What was the word for that? Anal. Still, she was a whole lot smarter than he'd ever be, with a high-level job—she'd probably have a new one in no time—to boot. Who was he to criticize her way of keeping track?

"If I put it on the list, it gets done," she continued. "If a task isn't in here, it could get pushed to another day, or forgotten altogether."

That made sense for a busy corporate executive. Speaking of busy, it was time to get that coffee and start work. "What's on that list for today?" he asked instead. He nodded at the brochures on the table. "Lined up any tours?"

She nodded. "Tate's Cranberry Factory at—" her attention dipped to the pint-size screen "—one-thirty."

"Interesting place. My sister and most of my friends work there. What else?"

"A beach walk this morning."

Nobody needed to write that down, but Nick wisely kept that opinion to himself. "That Palm Pilot is real important to you."

"I depend on it."

"So if it got lost or broken, you'd be stuck."

"I suppose I could switch to pen and paper if I had to." She flipped the gadget shut. "How do you keep track of your life?"

He never relied on written lists, not even if he wrote them out himself. Too much chance of misreading and screwing up. He pointed to his head. "It's all in here."

"Aren't you afraid you'll forget something?"

"Nope."

Her mouth opened and she looked ready to pry more into his life. She'd already skated way too close to his reading problems. He glanced meaningfully at the coffeepot. "Look, if I don't get my coffee and start work I'll be here till midnight."

He headed into the kitchen. Stopped and pivoted toward her. "What happens if something unexpected throws off your plans and keeps you from finishing that to-do list?"

"I'm a very organized person, Nick. If something unplanned pops up, I work around it."

She sounded like a vice president, capable and logical. Given the slight upward thrust of her chin, the light of self-assurance in her eyes and the slight I'm-in-control press of her full lips, she looked the part, too. Even her perfect neck seemed corporate.

Smart, cool, beautiful and way out of his league. How many times had he reminded himself of this, and why in hell did he want to kiss her more than ever?

He wanted more than that—her under him, control forgotten, lips pink with passion and eyes dark with need. His body stirred dangerously. He stifled a groan, or meant to. A soft, strangled sound wrenched from his throat.

Cinnamon's eyes widened. Her fingers gripped the Palm Pilot. For the second time, awareness colored and softened her features, opening her expression. He studied her face, let her see his interest.

This time she didn't look away. Her lips parted a fraction, and a rush of breath shot from between them. Nick recognized those signals, knew if he moved closer, leaned down and kissed her, she wouldn't stop him. She'd kiss him back, maybe more.

That scared him spitless. Getting involved with Cinnamon Smith was dangerous. Crazy, even. Not an option. Period.

Clearing his throat, he backed away. "I'll get my coffee now. And you ought to take that beach walk."

"Right. I'll go upstairs and grab my jacket." Cheeks flaming, she rushed toward the stairs.

As soon as she disappeared, Nick gave his brow a mental swipe and headed for the kitchen. He'd avoided kissing her. Barely.

What had come over him? Whatever it was it wouldn't happen again.

CINNAMON PICKED HER WAY around scattered driftwood and brittle sea grass as she returned to the Oceanside. Despite gloves her hands were cold, and her icy fingers sought warmth in the pockets of her parka. The knuckles of one hand brushed against the solid surface of her Palm Pilot, which she'd brought along for no particular reason and hadn't used. She could barely feel her toes or her nose and, despite a wool cap, her ears ached. But the pale winter sunshine, chilly sea air, whipping wind and brisk ocean waves exhilarated her. That feeling alone was worth the physical discomfort.

Entertained by the frothy ocean, seagulls and other birds, and the beachside cottages standing well back from the ocean, she'd walked longer and farther than planned. Now she barely had time for lunch before the tour at the cranberry factory.

She thought guiltily of her laptop, which she'd intended to put to use before the tour. No time for an online job search now. Later this afternoon or tonight, she promised herself.

As she neared the B and B she glanced at the driveway. There was no sign of Nick's truck. She wouldn't be seeing him, then. Her spirits plummeted, which irked her no end. For heaven's sake, she didn't even like the man.

Oh, no? Then what was this morning about? Nick had teased and charmed her with his devilish grin, his heavy-lidded, bad-boy eyes warming her wherever they lit. And who could resist a man with a tool belt hanging on his narrow hips and a healthy bulge below....

He was funny, nice and sexy. No wonder she had the hots for him. And how. She let out a dreamy sigh, then castigated herself with a scowl. No more of that. She was on a much-needed break from men. Besides, Nick wasn't the career-oriented, upwardly mobile, sophisticated male she wanted to share her life with. How many times must she remind herself?

Though he *was* single—a definite step up from Dwight.

Cinnamon braced for the familiar pain that always accompanied thoughts of her ex. But with the sea at her back, the Oceanside before her and a salty breeze tickling her face, the messy past seemed far away. To her relief, her heart continued to beat without aching, and her stomach remained unknotted. Fran had been wise, indeed, to invite her here.

Though nearly out of time to change and eat before the tour, she headed past the front door and around the far side of the veranda, unable to stop herself. On the blue tarp stood a worktable holding a large power saw and neatly arranged tools. There was a large gaping hole in the floor where wood planks had been ripped off. Nick wasn't through, after all. She'd see him later this afternoon, then, a cheery thought that lifted her spirits all too high.

Stern-faced—she would *not* think about Nick—Cinnamon spun around and marched to the front door. With fingers made clumsy from the cold, she fumbled the key into the lock, then opened the door and hurried inside.

The warmth of the house wrapped around her. She peeled off her gloves and glanced at her watch. If she didn't hurry, she'd be late. Better to eat in the car so as not to miss the tour.

With so much to do and think about, who had time to drool over a man she had no interest in? She shoved Nick Mahoney from her mind.

"YOU'LL LOVE ROSY'S Diner," Fran told Cinnamon as they ambled down the quiet sidewalk, past halogen streetlights and several parked cars. "It's a favorite among the locals. Great food at great prices." She licked her lips. "Wait'll you taste Rosy's home cooking."

"I can hardly wait." Cinnamon's stomach growled. "Since I pulled into your driveway last night, it seems as if I'm always hungry. I could gain ten pounds without half trying."

"I hope you do," Fran said with her trademark bluntness. "You're too thin."

"Stress-related weight loss." Her empty stomach growled again. "Leaving the city and coming here was exactly what I needed." She smiled at Fran.

"That's music to my heart." Fran studied her with a caring eye. "Already I see a difference in you. There's a healthy glow to your skin."

"Really?"

Only one thing marred Cinnamon's upbeat mood —the glaring item remaining on her to-do list. Looking for and landing a job. She'd meant to at least start the process, but after spending an afternoon at the factory and then driving around, she'd returned to the Oceanside scant minutes before Fran.

Of course, by then dusk had fallen, the hole in the veranda floor had been repaired and Nick had gone. She told herself she didn't care. Out of sight, out of mind. Which was true. She hadn't thought about him once since she and Fran had driven into town for dinner.

"Too bad you're not here during tourist season when the shops stay open at night," Fran said as they passed one- and two-story dark buildings. "It'd be fun to take you through some of our quirky shops."

"I'll come back tomorrow," Cinnamon said. After she looked for work.

The job search was crucial, something she could not afford to put off. Yet she'd done just that. Her guilty conscience dampened her spirits, followed by a jittery twinge. Well, the day wasn't over. She'd go online tonight before bed.

"There it is." Fran pointed to the pink, neon *Rosy's Diner* sign at the end of the block. A moment later she swung open the thick glass door and gestured Cinnamon in.

The typical blue-collar restaurant was noisy and crowded. Cinnamon and Fran hung their coats on the overloaded tree beside the door. As they headed for a vacant booth halfway across the room, waitresses and diners called out greetings to both Fran and Cinnamon.

Some even used her name, which surprised her. She shot Fran a puzzled look. "How do they know who I am?"

"We don't get a lot of visitors this time of year. That makes you big news."

"I don't know if I like that," she muttered.

"Nobody here bites, I swear. And they know nothing about your personal life."

She doubted she'd get the same warm reception if they did. If the people here were anything like her associates at Sabin and Howe, she'd likely be condemned and skewered for sleeping with her boss, who was still technically a married man.

They slid into an orange-cushioned booth angled with a view to the door. Cinnamon sniffed appreciatively. "Something sure smells good."

"What did I tell you? I highly recommend tonight's special, whatever it is. Here comes Rosy."

A short, wiry fiftyish waitress in support hose, clean white sneakers and a hot-pink uniform that matched the neon sign appeared at the table bearing two water glasses and napkin-wrapped silverware. She winked at Fran. "Hey there, sugarberry." Then she flashed a smile at Cinnamon. "You must be Cinnamon. Welcome to Cranberry. I'm Rosy."

Right off, Cinnamon liked this friendly woman. "It's good to meet you. I hear this is a great place to eat."

"The best in town," Fran added.

Without a trace of conceit, the diner owner nodded. "That's a fact. Course, I use the finest ingredients and old family recipes handed down from my great-great grandmamma, Soldano. I can give you a menu, or you can trust me and order tonight's special."

"That's what I told her," Fran said. "What is the special?"

"Spaghetti with clam sauce, garlic cheese bread and green salad with house dressing. For dessert, cranberry pound cake with hot fudge sauce."

Fran smacked her lips. "I'll have that, with a cup of coffee."

"Me, too," Cinnamon said.

The restaurant owner winked. "Smart girls. I'll be back with that coffee."

By the time Fran and Cinnamon unwrapped their silverware Rosy was back, steaming pot in hand. Cinnamon sampled her coffee, which was strong and surprisingly good.

Rosy moved to another table. "How was the factory tour?" Fran asked as she added sugar and milk to her mug.

"Interesting. I learned all about cranberries and how the juice is processed. The building and equipment are awfully run-down, though. No wonder the company's struggling." She shook her head.

"Don't get me started," Fran murmured. "You know that town council meeting that took up my afternoon? We spent a good part of it discussing that mess. We all agree, the downslide started eight years ago, when Randall Tate bought the business. Who knows why, since he lives in Chicago and owns a dozen companies headquartered in the Midwest."

She paused to taste her coffee. "When he bought the factory and retail store, both facilities needed upgrades and new equipment. Unfortunately, Tate never sank a dime into either. Today, bringing the place up to snuff would cost a fortune. Thanks to stiff competition, even if he did modernize, there's no guarantee of profits." She sighed. "No wonder nobody wants to buy the business."

"And if it doesn't sell?"

"The way things are going, the factory could close within six months." Fran cupped her mug as if the warmth from it could ward off the chilling thought. "Imagine ten percent of the population—207 men and women—searching for jobs in Cranberry, all at once." Worry darkened her face. "Sure, tourism is strong here, but we can't absorb that kind of unemployment."

With a grave expression Rosy slid the salads onto the table. "My business would suffer, too, especially during the off season. I can't afford that. We got to do something to save the factory."

"I know," Fran said. "That's why the mayor and town council have called an emergency meeting next Tuesday at 7:00 p.m. So spread the word."

Rosy brightened. "Now, that's something I can do."

As the waitress turned away, Fran frowned

thoughtfully at Cinnamon. "You work with struggling businesses. Maybe you can help."

"That is my field," Cinnamon said. "But the companies that hire me pay high fees for my expertise. At least, they did when I worked for Sabin and Howe. Seems to me, if the Tate Corporation wanted to hire a consultant, they would have by now."

"I hadn't thought about the fees." Fran glanced at her plate. "Suddenly I've lost my appetite. You want my salad?"

"Skipping dinner won't solve anything," Cinnamon pointed out. She stabbed a forkful of lettuce, artichoke heart and sunflower seeds. "You don't want to drop weight, like I did, and get too thin."

"I suppose you're right. Let's change the subject and talk about something else." Cinnamon's friend picked a cherry tomato from her plate and popped it into her mouth, chewing with relish. "How about my newly repaired veranda. Didn't Nick do a great job?"

She would have to mention him. Cinnamon wanted to groan. Instead she focused on her salad. "Since I don't know anything about carpentry, I don't have a clue whether he did a good job."

"He did. Believe me, the man is a genius. That veranda is fifty years old, with a tongue-and-groove floor. Replacing the rotted wood with boards that match the original takes skill and a ton of hard work. Nick even fashioned a special saw blade to do the job right. He's also fast and thorough. I'm lucky to have him." Fran paused to spear more salad. "He doesn't mind doing nonskilled labor, either. He's agreed to wash all the windows, and then prune the trees."

"Oh?" The news lifted Cinnamon's heart shamelessly, which bothered her no end. She didn't want to look forward to seeing Nick. "When will that be?"

"Tomorrow. There's a ton to do before Valentine's Day, so he'll be at the B and B every day for the next few weeks. You don't mind, do you?"

"Of course not." But every day? She wasn't sure she could handle seeing the man so often.

"Why the unhappy face?" Fran asked.

Because being around Nick is dangerous. He made her feel and want things she shouldn't, but Cinnamon wasn't about to voice her thoughts, not even to her best friend. "I'm curious. Besides working for you, what else does Nick do to earn his living?"

"Well," Fran began, tapping her fork thoughtfully against her lips, "he's good at fixing just about anything, and people hire him to do whatever they need. You know, repair broken toasters and washing machines, clean gutters, patch roofs. He's real good at making parts for old machines. He even patched up a machine or two at the cranberry factory, or so I hear."

"If he's that good, surely he could find full-time work."

"Oh, he's had offers. I don't think he wants to be tied down."

The very excuse Cinnamon's mother had voiced dozens of times to avoid working a regular job. Down that road lay poverty, a place Cinnamon refused ever again to visit. Further reason to avoid Nick, no matter how attractive he was. "I couldn't live like that," she said.

Fran shrugged. "He seems to have everything he needs."

The door opened, ushering in a blast of cold air Cinnamon felt halfway across the room. She glanced at the newcomers. A young girl in a turquoise parka and cream-colored scarf entered, followed by a woman in her mid-thirties, whom she recognized from the factory. The third person was Nick.

For once he wore a coat—a lined denim jacket that hugged his shoulders. His face was ruddy from the cold.

Her heart gave a joyful kick before she reined in her feelings. *He's not what I want,* she firmly reminded herself.

Fran aimed a canny stare her way. "Did you see who just walked in?"

"Yes, and don't look at me like that."

"Like what?" Fran's tone was pure innocence.

Suddenly Nick noticed her. His eyes widened a fraction and his expression was cool and unsmiling, as if he didn't want to see her, either. He glanced at her lips, which she realized had parted. She quickly compressed them. His eyes, now dark and hot, met hers, not in flirtation, but something deeper.

Fran and the noise in the room seemed to dim. Swallowing, Cinnamon reminded herself she didn't want Nick. Her body refused to listen. Her insides went haywire, melting and hungry, far worse than this morning. Lowering her gaze, barely conscious of her actions, she stabbed aimlessly at the last of her salad.

"They're coming this way," Fran murmured.

"Are they?"

Attention on her plate and every cell in her body alert, she waited.

Chapter Four

Cinnamon Smith was the last woman Nick wanted to see, especially after thinking about her the whole damn day. Thinking? Try fantasizing. About the way her eyes would light up when she saw him. Then, as he strode eagerly toward her, they would go dark with desire. Her soft body would mold to his. He'd take her mouth, cup her hips and…

And what was the point of wanting what never would be?

Yet the flare of pleasure in her eyes just now was real enough. His body jumped to attention just as it had in his fantasies, and he knew his eyes returned the same hungry expression. Suddenly her gaze jerked to her plate as if she'd dismissed him, making him wonder whether he'd imagined her interest out of wishful thinking.

He shoved his hands in his jacket pockets and cursed himself for bringing Sharon and Abby here to eat instead of some other place.

"There's Fran," Abby exclaimed, pushing her hair behind her ears in a pint-size but feminine gesture much like her mother's. "I can't wait to tell her about winning the practice math bee!"

She tried to walk but instead rushed forward, coltish legs skipping over the black-and-white linoleum.

Sharon, who was flushed with happiness over her daughter's unusually exuberant mood, laughed as she and Nick moved at a more leisurely pace. Since they knew everybody here, their progress slowed as they stopped to exchange greetings. Nick didn't mind—he needed the time to corral his randy feelings.

All too soon they neared Fran and Cinnamon's booth. He wanted to nod from a distance and leave things at that, but unfortunately the only empty booth was behind theirs, and the only way to reach it was to pass right by them. And with Abby already stationed there yammering away, he guessed he'd have to stop, too.

Nick glued a neutral expression on his face and stood between Sharon and his niece. Both Cinnamon and Fran were focused intently on the girl, which took some of the stress off the moment and allowed him to study Cinnamon without her knowing. Her cheeks were a good deal rosier than they were this morning. Sun or windburn, he figured, liking the color.

By the amused gleam in her eyes, she enjoyed listening to Abby, whose excitement seemed to bubble out of her.

"It was just the practice bee," she was saying. "But I won!"

As she paused for breath, Nick nodded at Fran and Cinnamon. "Is Abby bothering you?"

"Are you kidding?" Fran grinned fondly at her. "I love this girl, and I am so proud of her."

Abby beamed, and Nick's heart seemed to swell in his chest. He was proud of her, too, and it felt good, seeing her happy.

"You must be great at math," Cinnamon said, lips curling and eyes crinkling at the corners. "That talent will take you far in life."

Nick had never seen that warm, carefree grin before. Apparently, a full day in Cranberry had worked wonders of her mood. Without the worry lines and shadows in her eyes, she looked younger and prettier than ever. Beautiful, even. Forgetting himself, he drank her in, feeling as though he could watch her all night.

He stared until Sharon nudged him and he remembered his manners. Clearing his throat, he made the introductions. "This is Abby's mom, my sister, Sharon. Meet Cinnamon Smith, a friend of Fran's."

Cinnamon extended her hand the way she probably did all the time in the corporate world. "Pleased to meet you," she said, sounding sincere.

Nick's sister looked startled—people didn't often shake hands with her. The handshake went off without a hitch—a small thing, yet, judging by Sharon's newly confident expression, important.

"I saw you at the factory this afternoon," his sister said. "I was the one in the shower cap, tending the sorter." She self-consciously fingered the clip that held her shoulder-length hair back at the nape.

Cinnamon nodded. "I remember. I was impressed by how seriously you took your job."

"Thanks for noticing." For an instant Sharon stood taller. Then her shoulders sagged. "Though the way things are going lately, I don't think it matters much what I do there."

Had she forgotten their decision to keep the factory troubles from Abby? Nick sent his sister a warning frown and cocked his chin his niece's way. Sharon closed her mouth.

Oblivious to the exchange, Abby remained focused on Cinnamon, taking in her expensive, dark green turtleneck sweater, the classy pearl studs in her ears and her tastefully painted lips with admiring eyes and an open mouth. In a word, she looked starstruck. Sharon seemed equally impressed.

Why that irked Nick was beyond him. Then again, like it or not, he was just as intrigued.

"Tomorrow night, my Mom, Uncle Nick and I are driving to Portland," Abby announced. "We're staying at a motel and everything! Then Friday morning I compete in the real math bee." Her excitement dimmed. "I hope I win."

Nick cupped her thin shoulder and gently squeezed. "You will, kid."

"I'll bet your Uncle Nick is right on the money," Cinnamon encouraged.

Briefly her eyes locked with his, and he saw that she truly wanted his niece to succeed. That made him like her all the more.

He didn't want to care the way he did, and they'd said their hellos. Time to head to their own table. "You get all the stuff on your list done?" he asked instead.

"Except for the job search."

The pinched, tense expression returned to Cinnamon's face, making him wished he hadn't said anything.

"You're out of work?" Sharon sighed with the sympathy of a woman soon to be in the same boat. "I didn't realize."

"Cinnamon is a talented woman," Fran said. "She'll find something soon."

"Of course I will," Cinnamon stated, but her assured tone and raised chin and didn't quite mask her underlying anxiety.

Any fool could see how worried she was, including Abby. Her own face sobered. "Miss Smith?"

"That sounds so formal. Please, call me Cinnamon."

"Cinnamon. My uncle Nick taught me how to relax so my mind can work and do what it needs to." Abby glanced up at him, her eyes shining. "That's how I won the practice math bee. You could try that when you look for a job."

"Thanks for the tip."

Cinnamon's mouth twitched, but as she glanced at Nick her eyebrows arched in curiosity and something more. He wasn't sure, but he thought she admired him for his advice to the kid.

Damned if his cheeks didn't burn. He shifted his weight and offered an aw-shucks shrug.

"Uncle Nick can teach you how to relax," Abby said. "It's not hard at all, you just breathe and tell yourself to stop worrying. It really works, too." Every part of her bounced up and down, even her hair. She turned to Nick. "You can teach her right now!"

Him, a man who could barely read, teach anything to Cinnamon, an educated executive? Unless she wanted to know how to make a machine part out of scrap, not likely. Now, with her, Fran, Abby and Sharon all staring at him, he felt awkward and out-of-place. He rubbed the back of his neck, wondering how to get out of this.

Luckily, just then Rosy showed up balancing two steaming plates. "Whatever Nick was going to teach you will have to wait, because dinner has arrived," she announced as she deftly placed the plates in front of

Cinnamon and Fran. "And we all know my food tastes best while it's hot. Enjoy, girls."

Nick released a relieved breath. "Come on, let's let them eat in peace," he said, gesturing Sharon and Abby to the empty booth.

"Nice meeting you, Abby, and good luck Friday," Cinnamon said. "Good to meet you, too, Sharon."

His sister brightened with pleasure. "You're here for two weeks, right? I hope to see you again."

"I'd like that."

Puzzled, Nick frowned. His single-mom, high-school-grad sister and the college-educated Cinnamon were as different as plastic and copper tubing, yet they seemed to like each other.

"See you tomorrow, Nick," Fran said. "Even if it ra—"

Rosy silenced her with a no-nonsense look. "What'd I say about eating your food while it's hot?" She glanced meaningfully at Nick and Sharon. "I may as well take your orders now, but you gotta sit down first."

Nick could have hugged the restaurant owner for putting an end to the conversation. Sliding into the booth, his back to the two women to better push Cinnamon from his mind, he focused on Rosy.

"What's the special tonight?"

HUNCHED AGAINST THE DRIVING rain, toolbox tucked protectively under his arm, Nick took the Oceanside steps two at a time. No surprise that yesterday's sun-shine had given way to the usual January rain. He wouldn't be tree pruning or washing windows today. Everybody knew he was driving Sharon and Abby to Portland later. He could have taken the morning off and stayed home, but Fran expected him, and he needed the work.

Icy breath huffed from his lips and, despite dashing from the truck to the stairs, his hands were wet and cold. Under the shelter of the veranda, he swiped his palms on the thighs of his jeans, then clomped across the veranda to check his work from yesterday. Though the entire floor needed a power wash and a coat of sealer, for now it would do.

Yesterday morning Cinnamon was sitting at the table, sipping coffee, and as he pivoted toward the sliding doors, expectation made his heart thud from more than taking the stairs two at a time.

She wasn't there. Disappointment sluiced through him, as unwelcome as the icy water trickling down the back of his collar. No matter how hard he tried he couldn't push her out of his thoughts. Sternly he scraped his boots on the mat. Well, she'd never know. Nobody would.

The slider was unlocked. He stepped inside.

"Good morning, Nick," Fran called from the kitchen. Scooping up two steaming mugs, she carried them into the dining room, indicating she wanted to start his day with friendly chitchat. That was her way, and he was okay with it.

"This is fresh-brewed and extra-strong, the way you like it," she said.

He set his toolbox on the floor, then accepted a mug. "Thanks." Heat from the drink seeped into his fingers, and the fragrant steam warmed his nose. "It's a nasty one today."

"So I see." She gestured him into a seat at the table, then sat down across from him. "I told Cinnamon to skip her morning run, but she insisted."

So that's where she was. Nick scoffed. "What is she, nuts?"

"Disciplined and stubborn. Since college, every Tuesday, Thursday and Saturday, rain, snow or shine, she does her three miles." Frowning, Fran glanced at her watch. "She left about ten minutes ago, heading for the road. I'm surprised you didn't see her."

Other than a few vehicles cautiously picking their way through the driving rain, Nick had seen no one. "This is flu season, and with the cold and rain... What was she thinking?"

"Believe me, I tried to talk her out of this." Fran shrugged. "Keeping to a schedule is as important to her as your toolbox is to you." Leaning forward as if sharing a secret, she added, "She had a chaotic childhood, and I think the order that comes from a schedule makes her feel in control."

"Huh." Nick wasn't sure he understood, not when sticking to a schedule meant jogging in the freezing rain.

"That's one reason why resigning from Sabin and Howe has been so difficult for her," Fran continued. "The schedule she relied on for years no longer works."

"I thought she was laid off," he said, frowning. "Why would she resign? Was the company doing something illegal?"

"No. Dwight Sabin—" She cut herself off. "I promised Cinnamon I wouldn't tell."

Nick wanted to know, but what had happened was none of his business. He turned his attention to his coffee, and for a moment the only sound was the battering rain.

"You heard about the emergency town council meeting a week from tonight?" Fran asked seconds later.

He nodded. "Sharon and I'll be there." He met her gaze, letting his worry show. "Do you think we'll be able to keep the factory from closing?"

"Not without help," she said, her face as bleak as the gray day. "You know, Cinnamon works with companies in trouble. She's saved more than a few from going under."

"No kidding." Hope stirred in Nick's chest. "Think she can help us?"

"I don't know. She doesn't come cheap, and I doubt the Tate company will pay."

Given their skinflintish behavior so far, that was likely true. His spirits fell.

"Think I'll bring her to the meeting, though. You never know."

"You never do," he agreed, but he didn't expect anything.

Neither of them spoke, each lost in dismal thoughts. Though Nick never wanted to work at the factory—he didn't want to work for anybody but himself—he couldn't imagine Cranberry without it. Where would all the laid-off workers, Sharon and friends among them, find work? His sister might be forced to move away, taking Abby with her.

Nick hated the thought, and wasn't sure he could handle that. But Cranberry was his home and he'd never leave. He felt comfortable in the small town, liked knowing his neighbors well enough that if they got too close, he could tell them to shove off and know that if he needed them they'd still be around. But without Sharon and Abby...

Tired of thinking about what might happen, and suddenly antsy, he glanced at the clock over the stove. "I'm leaving early today, so I should get started. What do you want me to do?"

Fran's eyes widened as she, too, noted the time. "Heavens, it's late, and I've got a bajillion errands to run. Since you can't wash the outside windows, how about the inside? I took down the curtains and loaded them into the car for dry-cleaning. Also, the upstairs hallway and bedrooms need paint touch-ups. You'll find leftover paint in the garage."

Nick shook his head. "Wall color changes as it ages. I'll chip off paint from each room and ask the hardware store to match it."

"I hadn't thought of that," Fran mused. She smiled. "Smart thinking, Nick."

He shrugged off the words. He'd learned through experience, was all. "Anything else?"

"The garage door squeaks when it opens and closes. And the ceiling fan in the Orca suite isn't working, but since it won't be used till summer, there's no hurry on that."

"May as well do it today, if Cinnamon doesn't mind me in her room."

"I told her about the windows, so she knows you'll be up there."

Even so, working in her bedroom seemed like a breach of privacy. "I'd like to ask her myself," Nick said. If she ever got back. He glanced out at the wind-whipped ocean and its frothing waves. "You shouldn't have let her go."

"What was I supposed to do, handcuff her and tie her to the dining room table?"

An image of Cinnamon wearing skimpy lingerie,

writhing seductively as she tried to work her way out of handcuffs filled his head. His body stirred, but he doubted Fran saw the scenario the same way he did. Shaking his head, he banished the fantasy. "You think she'll make it back all right?"

Looking thoughtful, Fran stood, and so did Nick. "I do, but if she's not back in another ten minutes..."

"I'll go out and find her, then bawl her out for sticking to a schedule that makes no sense."

Fran's mouth twitched. "I'd like to see that."

Chapter Five

Freezing rain pummeled Cinnamon as she sprinted across the Oceanside's driveway. Despite the micro-fiber jogging suit, gloves and socks she wore for warmth and water resistance, she was both wet and cold. And—thanks to soaked sneakers and slippery ground—suffering the dull ache that preceded shin splints. At least she'd finished the route she'd traced yesterday, driving the distance to make sure it was three miles.

Worse than physical discomfort was the sight of Nick's truck parked beside her car. After spending a restless night lusting over the man—feelings she intended to keep firmly in check—she wasn't up to facing him today.

She'd meant to get back, shower and leave before he showed up, but wouldn't you know, he'd arrived much earlier today than yesterday. Apparently, the man didn't have a regular schedule, but then, she knew that. Disapproval puffed from her lips in a cold cloud.

And dread. No doubt with her wet hair and red face, she looked disastrous, even less put-together than the night they'd met. But there was nothing to be done about that now.

Spent, gasping for breath, she was eager to reach the warmth of the house. She would simply rush upstairs and avoid Nick. Near the top of the outside steps she slipped on the slick surface, whacking her shin hard. Pain exploded in her lower leg.

"Ow, ow!" she howled in panting gasps. Tears filled her vision. Crying wouldn't help, and blinking furiously, she sank heavily onto the step, which was sheltered by the eaves. Teeth clenched, she gripped her thigh with the fingers of her soaked gloves, as if that would stem the agony. Of course it didn't. Neither did the cold seeping into her behind.

After a moment the pain subsided a little and she mustered the courage to examine the injury. First, though, she divested her icy hands of the gloves. Slowly and carefully—mustn't touch the shin—she inched her pant leg upward with stiff fingers. Despite her care, cold water dribbled over the tender skin, stinging as it connected with the bloody, two-inch gash.

Chilled and shivering, she moaned, the sound drowned out by the pounding rain. Blood trickled down her leg—better than the flood it might have been. Already the area around the cut was puffy and red, sure signs of the nasty bruise to come.

Tremors shook her and her teeth chattered. Pain or not, she couldn't sit here any longer or she'd freeze to death. She rolled her pant leg up to the knee. Clutching the railing, she hauled herself up. Dizzy from pain or maybe shock, she stood where she was and waited for her head to clear. Then, using the wood siding for support, she limped to the front door.

Of course, it was locked. Fran had left the dining room sliding door unlocked, both for Nick and for her. But that was at a good fifteen feet away. Cold and hurting as she was, Cinnamon didn't think she could make it that far.

Nothing to do but ring the bell. Leaning her shoulder against the doorjamb, stifling the urge to scream, she waited.

It seemed like forever before Nick opened the door.

"About time you showed up." His brow creased in an unfamiliar frown that turned his face stern and forbidding. "I was about to come looking for you to make sure you hadn't fallen into a hole someplace. Here." He thrust a bath towel at her.

The last thing she wanted was a lecture, especially from Nick. The towel, however, was another matter. "You're not the boss of me," she snapped.

As she snatched the towel, her weight shifted to the injured leg. Crying out in pain, she fell against the open door.

Strong hands caught her, and the towel slipped from her grasp.

"What happened to *you?*"

She sighed, feeling ridiculous. "I slipped on the steps and banged up my shin. It's nothing, really." She tried to summon a smile of reassurance but couldn't manage it through her chattering teeth.

A worried look replaced Nick's frown. "My God, you're freezing to death." He toed the towel out of the way, then kicked the door shut. "Give me that jacket and sit down," he ordered, guiding her onto a nearby bench.

Before she registered the words he deftly unzipped her windbreaker and peeled it off. The long-sleeved T-shirt underneath was nearly as wet.

Nick glanced at her breasts. "Soaked clean through," he muttered. He jerked his gaze upward, his eyes flashing both heat and anger. "What in hell were you thinking?"

"I needed the exercise—"

He swore. "What you need is a dose of common sense. And you, with all that education. You got a bathrobe in your room? Because you can't stay in that shirt." Face dark, he glanced at her sopped legs. "Or those pants."

The disapproving tone chafed. Cinnamon struggled to her feet—or tried.

Nick gently but firmly pushed her back down.

Who was this bossy male? She scowled up at him. "I want to take my shower now, so please —"

"Stay put." Snatching the towel from the floor, he draped it around her shoulders. A glance at her shin and he shook his head. "I don't want you catching a cold and blaming me. I'll be back with your robe." He started up the stairs.

No one had ever taken care of Cinnamon. For as long as she could remember, she'd looked after herself as well as her mother. Used to being in charge, she wasn't sure she liked Nick in that role. "Once I shower and warm up I'll be fine," she insisted.

"I'll be the judge of that. Don't move."

His gaze held her as sure as hands, and she nodded. "Okay."

The moment he disappeared she glanced at her chest. Wouldn't you know, her sports bra did nothing to conceal her cold nipples poking against her wet shirt. That explained the hot look in Nick's eyes.

Mortified, she crossed her arms—since he was upstairs, a useless action. Well, he wouldn't see anything else. Forget the robe and meekly sitting here. She'd dry off and head upstairs, even if she had to scoot on her behind to get there.

CINNAMON TOWELED HER hair, then set to work removing her shoes and socks—a difficult task that took longer than she thought, given that they were wet, her shin ultrasensitive and her hands clumsy with cold. Unfortunately, before she peeled off the second sock, Nick was back with her robe, a formless, navy flannel knee-length thing she wore when nobody else was around. Too bad she hadn't brought her sexy, peach-colored satin robe instead.

Right. As if she'd wear that in front of Nick. Not that she wanted to model the shapeless robe for him, either.

One hand hugging the now-damp towel to her chest, she used the other to grasp the back of the bench and stand. "I don't need the robe. I'm going up-stairs."

"Are you nuts?" His jaw tightened stubbornly. "First you change and warm up."

Dizzy with pain and too distraught to argue, she sank down, still hugging the towel to her breasts.

"That's better."

Nothing to do but change into the robe. Cinnamon held out her free hand. "I'll take that, thanks."

"Wet as you are now? Uh-uh." Holding the garment out of reach, he glanced at the towel. "Better strip first."

What!? "Excuse me?"

He released an exasperated breath. "I won't look. Just get out of those clothes." Slinging the robe over his shoulder, he eyed her.

By his feet—planted firmly in front of her—and his stony expression, she knew he wouldn't budge until she complied. "Turn around," she said. Using the back of the bench for support, she pulled herself up.

"I'm glad you finally came to your senses." He turned his back to her. "I'll toss this to you when you're ready."

"Close your eyes," she ordered.

"What for? I can't see out of the back of my head."

"I don't care. Close your eyes."

"Brother," he grumbled, followed by a muttered string of words she couldn't decipher. "All right, they're closed."

"Thank you." Acutely aware of his presence, she tugged the soaked shirt over her head. Her wet bra followed, and both dropped onto the bench. Leaning her shoulder against the wall, she attempted to tug her dripping pants over her hips with one hand. The wet microfiber clung stubbornly to her skin, and the movement caused her rolled-up pant leg to fall. The fabric brushed her shin, and excruciating pain spiked up her leg. A taut breath hissed from her lips.

"Cinnamon?" Nick started to turn around.

"Don't you dare move, Nick Mahoney. I'm half-naked!"

Uttering a strangled sound, he froze. "Are you or are you not all right?"

He sounded angry, which puzzled her. "My pant leg brushed my shin, and it really hurt. And now," she began shyly, "I'm afraid to take off my pants."

"I suppose you want me to do it," he growled.

The thought of Nick helping with something so intimate emptied her brain of a reply.

"I'll take your silence as a yes." He sounded even more exasperated. "But I won't turn around till you put on your robe." Raising his hand he lobbed it backward over his shoulder, right into her outstretched arm.

"Thanks." She slipped into the flannel robe and tied the sash. The fabric felt warm, soft and unbelievably sensual against her cold, sensitive nipples.

"Safe to turn around now?"

"Yes," she said, hastily pulling the lapels together.

Nick pivoted toward her. His dark eyes fell to her mouth, then dipped to her hand at the vee of her robe. Wordlessly, he hunkered down before her.

Under different circumstances a man at her feet would have been romantic and suggestive. Wet, unwashed and probably reeking, her pants half down her hips, she was anything but attractive. No doubt Nick was wondering how he got stuck sharing yet another mortifying moment of her life.

"Hold on to my shoulders," he said.

He was wearing a black T-shirt, not much protection against the dead of winter. Yet under her cold hands he felt warm. And solid, from hard, physical labor. Not much fat on this man.

He reached for her waistband and started to tug down. Cinnamon tensed. "Be careful of my shin," she warned.

Hesitating, he glanced up at her, his face a mask of doubt. "Did I hurt you?"

"No." Acutely embarrassed, she glanced at his fingers, hooked inside her waistband and bikini panties. "Um, I'll keep my panties on."

"And here I thought I was about to get you totally naked." For the first time, his mouth quirked, a cockeyed grin that softened the moment. "Ready?"

Cinnamon nodded. For a big man he was surprisingly gentle. As he coaxed the reluctant fabric down her thighs and somehow cleared her injured shin his muscles bunched under her palms, and the clean smells of soap and man filled her senses.

Despite her throbbing shin the rest of her jolted to life. Desire filled her, and she barely managed to keep from tangling her fingers through his thick, black hair, leaning down and kissing him.

After what seemed like decades, the pants pooled at her feet. Tightening her grip on Nick's shoulders she lifted her injured leg while he carefully tugged the pants over her heels and off.

The hem of the robe fell into place. Gratitude didn't come easily. "Thank you, Nick." She bit her lip and sat down.

"Anytime," he quipped, still hunkered at her feet. "Now, let's see that shin." He cupped her foot in his warm, callused hands and raised her leg a fraction. "Ouch," he said, frowning at the ugly wound. "You might have broken something, or maybe you need stitches."

He released her foot. Instantly, she missed his warmth.

"I don't think so," Cinnamon said, hoping she was right. "The cut isn't deep, and the rest is just a bad bruise."

"You should see a doctor," Nick insisted.

Which would put a bigger dent in her carefully planned day. She shook her head. "What I need is a shower, a cup of coffee and my laptop."

"Laptop?" He frowned. "I thought you looked for a job last night when you got home."

"I started." She'd checked her e-mail, disappointed to discover not one reply from the host of colleagues she'd e-mailed. So she'd resent the messages, then, exhausted and discouraged, had collapsed in bed. "I planned on doing more today, and also browsing some of the shops."

"Plans change," Nick said. "You can take that shower, but if you want coffee, you'll drink it in the car. We're going to Doc Bartlett's."

Cinnamon rolled her eyes, which only tightened Nick's determined expression.

"If your Dr. Bartlett is like most doctors he's probably booked weeks in advance," she argued. "I can't just barge in."

"You can at Doc's. I'll help you upstairs," he said,

gently pulling her to her feet. "While you clean up, I'll make that appointment."

"If you must," she conceded unhappily.

His arm circled her waist and they started up the steps. She tried to hold herself aloof, but, cradled in his solid warmth, she quickly melted, leaning gratefully against him. Her head settled in the comfortable indentation where his arm and shoulder met, and she let out a sigh. Pain aside, she felt small and wonderfully coddled—a thought that stiffened her posture.

As soon as she tensed, Nick stilled, chin angled and eyes on hers. "You okay? If not, I could carry you the rest of the way up." One eyebrow raised, and the corner of his mouth quirked.

Because the idea appealed to her, she frowned and tried to pull out of his grasp. "I don't need your help."

His arm remained around her waist. "Too bad, because I'm not going away."

SQUINTING THROUGH GOLD-RIMMED bifocals and stroking his neatly trimmed, snow-white beard, Doc Bartlett silently considered the X-ray that hung on the wall of the exam room. Standing beside Cinnamon, who sat on the exam table with her legs outstretched, Nick, too, scrutinized the image. Not that he knew what he was looking at, other than her shin.

He doubted she knew, either, though she studied the thing with the same intensity as Doc. But unlike the calm doctor, tension pinched her mouth, and fine lines creased the normally smooth place between her eyebrows. Even her hands looked anxious, pleating her skirt. Pain and nerves, Nick guessed. And maybe, owing to her above-the-knee skirt and bare legs, cold.

Not the best way to dress in the winter, but better than cutting the leg off a pair of her expensive slacks or designer jeans. The skirt showed off her slim, shapely legs. That didn't help her, but Nick appreciated the view—except for the angry-looking wound in the center of her right shin.

The sight made his gut hurt. He wished he could comfort her, something he'd tried when Doc had cleaned the wound. Cinnamon had cried out and gripped Nick's hand so hard, he'd winced. The minute Doc had finished, she'd let go and had balled her hands into white-knuckled fists, proving that he didn't know beans about soothing her.

Well, playing nursemaid never had been his strong suit and wasn't his job. He was here because he'd had no choice but to bring her.

Which was a load of crap. Truth was, he wanted to be here with her, even if it meant spending a long time in Doc's office.

An hour and a half ago he would've denied that, honestly believing he'd conquered his attraction. But her accident had changed everything. The beautiful, competent Cinnamon Smith needed him, and the novelty of that had sucked the marrow right out of his resolve.

The wet T-shirt under her worthless jacket hadn't helped, either. One look at her taut nipples and he forgot that he shouldn't want her. Then later, knowing she was topless under her robe and wearing only her panties had about killed him. And her hands grasping his shoulders and her warm breath brushing his face… Cold hands and all, who knew what a turn-on that would be?

Then putting his hands on her hips and stripping off her pants, his face inches from the apex of her thighs—sweet torture.

Dog that he was, he'd wanted her then, bloody shin and all. Unfortunately, over the past hour that hadn't changed.

He shook his head in self-disgust. Thank God, Cinnamon didn't have a clue. She never would, either. From now on he'd keep his eyes above her shoulders, his hands to himself and his mind out of the gutter.

Suddenly she looked at him, telegraphing unease in those big, cinnamon-color eyes. Forgetting his newly made resolve, he reached for her, just as Doc turned from the X-ray.

Saved by the doctor's attention, Nick jerked back. Eyes narrowed a fraction, Doc shot him a shrewd look, his white hair and beard making him look like Santa Claus, only without the belly and red suit.

Nick didn't want the old man getting ideas, so he crossed his arms and pasted a carefully neutral expression on is face. "What's the verdict?"

Doc smiled at both of them. "You'll be pleased to know, nothing's broken. No hairline fractures, either."

"That's good news." Cinnamon released a sigh of relief.

So did Nick. She wouldn't need a cast, and at last he could drive her back to the Oceanside. He'd help her get settled and then start on his chores. Which, since he had to leave early, he'd barely be able to start, much less finish.

Holding her skirt in place with one hand Cinnamon scooted toward the end of the table, wincing as she moved.

"Where do you think you're going?" Doc asked, his kindly face now as stern as a Baptist minister preaching about sin.

"I can't leave?" she asked hopefully.

"Not till I stitch up that gash." He frowned at the gaping wound, which had started to bleed again.

The color drained from her face. "Do I really need stitches?"

"Unless you want a scar on that pretty leg."

Nobody asked, but in Nick's opinion, no scar could ruin her leg.

"I don't want that." She swallowed nervously. "It's just, it hurts so much when anything touches it." Her hands started a fresh round of fidgeting. "The thought of stitches…" The words trailed off, and Nick worried she might pass out.

Doc gave a sympathetic nod. "I can give you something for the pain."

"And I'll hold your hand again, if you promise not to break my fingers," Nick teased, hoping to coax a smile.

Instead he earned a frown that smarted like a slap and sent a clear message: she no longer needed him. Time to get out of here.

He backed away from the table. "Look, I'll wait outside."

"I would if I were you," Cinnamon said without much enthusiasm.

Was that a silent plea in her eyes? Did she want him by her side after all, or was that wishful thinking? Wishful thinking, he figured. As he opened the door, he glanced at the doctor. "Come get me when you're through."

Hands in his pockets, he wandered past two exam rooms, both with patients ready for Doc, into the spacious waiting room. This morning there were only two adults there, which didn't surprise Nick since nowadays most people used the clinic outside town. He preferred the family doctor who'd seen him, Sharon and Abby through injuries and all the childhood stuff his niece had caught and shared. Doc's friendly manner put Nick at ease. Also, he liked getting appointments right away.

What he didn't like was seeing Liz Jessup on the sofa near the fish tank. As always, she was decked out in seductive clothes, this time a low-cut, clingy sweater, a tight, short skirt, diamond-patterned hose and heels so high he wondered how she walked in them.

A man couldn't help appreciating her big breasts and round behind, but she wasn't Nick's type. Years back, the then thirty-something divorcée and single mom had hired him to fix her washing machine. Though Nick was ten-plus years her junior, she'd propositioned him more than once. Since he wasn't attracted, he'd turned her down every time. Plenty of other men were interested, and she had her pick of dates. Word was, she wanted a husband, but so far no man had gone there. In the meantime she'd never stopped trying to seduce Nick.

Careful to keep his eyes off her impressive cleavage, he bypassed the sofa for a less comfortable ladder-back chair. He took the seat beside Bill Patterson, a whale-size man who'd retired from the cranberry factory several years earlier.

"Morning." He nodded to both of them.

"Hey, Nick," Bill returned, hooking his thumbs through his trademark cranberry-red suspenders.

Liz fluttered lashes so long and black they had to

be fakes, tossed her thick, wavy hair sexily and curved her red lips into a smile. "Well, hello, there." She crossed her legs, a move that revealed a long slice of thigh. "What are you doing here? I hope Abby's not sick, not with that math bee tomorrow."

Her legs were nice, but nothing like Cinnamon's.

Nick explained about the accident, while Bill, Liz and Audrey Eames, the plump, fifty-something receptionist-nurse behind the check-in station, listened attentively.

"I heard Cinnamon was at Rosy's last night," Liz commented. "What's she like?"

Bill nodded that he, too, wondered. "The one night I decided to eat in," he muttered.

Their interest came as no surprise. Winters in Cranberry were dark, slow times, and they were curious about the only outsider in town.

"She's okay," he said hedged.

Okay? More like sexy and beautiful, just about the classiest woman he ever had met. Way classier than he'd ever be.

"That doesn't tell us much." Liz shook her head at the tile ceiling. "Men."

"I met her when she checked in," Audrey said.

"Yeah?" Patting the cushion, Liz gestured her over. "Tell us about her."

"Guess I can, for a minute." The receptionist-nurse left her station, talking as she joined them. "She's a pretty little thing, average height, and slender. Huge eyes and a black, spiky hairstyle that looks real cute on her."

Liz nodded, then glanced from man to man. "That's the kind of stuff a woman wants to know."

Audrey sat down beside her, then turned her attention on Nick. "What do you know about her as a person? We want details."

At Nick's blank look, Bill grinned and shook his head. "Better tell 'em something or they'll nag you to death."

Probably true. Nick shrugged. "I don't know that much, except that she's a former corporate executive looking for work."

"And she thinks she'll find it here?" Audrey tsked and shook her head.

"Not with Tate's in trouble," Bill said.

"Big trouble," Liz seconded with a worried frown. Her brother and nineteen-year-old son worked there, one in shipping and the other in processing.

"Cinnamon isn't looking for work here," Nick said. "She only came to visit Fran. They're old friends." He eyed Audrey. "Satisfied?"

"Not really."

Not about to say more, Nick set his jaw.

Sighing, the receptionist gave up. "But I guess it'll have to do." The phone rang, and she hurried back to her station.

In no mood for further conversation, Nick picked up a magazine and pointedly opened it, beyond caring that he couldn't read it.

Chapter Six

Half an hour later, cupping Cinnamon's elbow, Doc slowly walked her into the waiting room. "She's all yours, Nick."

Ignoring curious looks from Liz and Bill, he tossed aside the magazine and stood.

"Take care, young lady," Doc said. "If you change your mind about crutches or that pain medication, call me."

"I don't think I will, thank you," she said.

As Nick moved to her side, Audrey bustled off to ready the room for another patient. "Take care, hon," she called out in a pleasant voice, "and hope to see you again—only not here."

"Definitely not here," Cinnamon replied with a polite smile.

Nick grasped her arm as Doc had, but she brushed off his hand, her smile abruptly gone. "I'm okay."

Stung and forgetting that he didn't want to touch her anyway, he dropped his hand.

"What were you reading?" she asked, shooting a curious glance at the magazine he'd tossed aside.

"Nothing." Past ready to get back to the Oceanside, he jerked his chin toward the door. "Let's go."

She squinted at the magazine. "*Entrepreneur.* I read that issue a few months back. Did you see the article on building up your—"

"Liz, your room's ready," Audrey called from the hall.

"Be right there." The divorcée stood and sashayed toward Cinnamon. "I'm Liz Jessup, an old friend of Nick's."

Winking at him as if they shared a secret, she touched his biceps. Nick sidestepped away from her.

Ignoring the rebuff, she smiled at Cinnamon, who extended her hand the same as she'd done with Sharon. "Pleased to meet you."

"Likewise. I manage a store called Cranberries-to Go, at the far end of Main Street. Be sure to stop in."

"I noticed your shop, and had planned to come in this afternoon." She glanced at the rectangular bandage covering her shin and offered a wry smile. "Not anymore."

"Too bad," Liz said. "Sorry about your accident."

"I'll be fine," Cinnamon insisted, "And I *will* stop by your shop tomorrow."

Nick shook his head at that. Unless her leg felt a whole lot better she wouldn't be driving anyplace for a while. He wouldn't be around to help her tomorrow, either, as he'd be in Portland, rooting for Abby at the math bee. Fran would have to chauffeur her.

"Well, time for my annual checkup." Liz winked. "I'll watch for you tomorrow, Cinnamon." She waved her scarlet nails at Bill, then blew Nick a kiss. "'Bye, hon." Wiggling her hips seductively, she strutted toward the exam rooms.

"She's pretty, in a dancehall-girl way," Cinnamon noted, shooting him a look he couldn't decipher.

He shrugged. "I guess."

From his seat, Bill cleared his throat. "I'm Bill Patterson. I'd get up but I had hip surgery a while back and the darn thing's still stiff as a piece of driftwood."

Expression sympathetic, Cinnamon nodded. "I hope it feels better soon. I'd come over and shake your hand but…" She glanced at her leg.

"Aren't we a pair, now." If Bill's grin grew any wider his mouth would split, a sign that Cinnamon had charmed him. He glanced at her shin. "What'd Doc do to you?"

"X-ray and stitches, but they're the dissolving kind, so I don't have to come back."

"Lucky you. I had stitches, too. Mine itched like a son of a gun. Don't scratch 'em or you might need new ones."

"Thanks for the tip."

At this rate they'd never leave. Nick cleared his throat. "Can we go now?"

His less-than-thrilled tone must have surprised Cinnamon, for her eyes widened. "Right away. 'Bye, Bill."

"Hope to see you again. Good luck finding a job."

Her startled gaze darted to Nick. By now she was easy to read, and he noted her displeasure with surprise of his own. Her unemployment was no secret, so he shrugged and shuttled her out.

WALKING UNASSISTED TOWARD the door of Doc's office required concentration, and Cinnamon didn't try to make conversation. Nick, too, was silent, which was fine by her, since at the moment she didn't want to talk to him. Awful enough he'd half undressed her and then been stuck with driving her here. She'd also squeezed the life from his fingers like a helpless little thing, something her mother might have done.

Cinnamon cringed. She hated weakness, and had spent her whole adult life suppressing anything that resembled it. Yet this was the second time Nick had seen her at her most vulnerable. He must think her an emotional mess. Compared to blond, sexy Liz she looked a physical wreck, too.

Nick opened the door and she limped slowly outside. The driving rain had turned into a cold mist that bit at her face and legs despite the covered walkway. Shivering, she pulled her jacket close.

"Cold?" He slanted her the same worried look she'd seen in the exam room.

She nodded.

"I'd give you my jacket if I had it. You'll warm up in the truck," he said, gesturing at the vehicle parked about thirty feet away. "Wait here and I'll bring it around like I did before."

He strode forward, his legs rapidly covering the distance. He moved with an easy grace that made watching him enjoyable. Like all trucks, his required a big step up to reach the cab, even with his long legs. He hopped into his seat, and a moment later the engine purred to life.

Parking within a few feet of her, he leaned over and opened the passenger door. His raised eyebrows told her he was ready to help, but she tightened her mouth and narrowed her eyes, warning him off. He stayed in his seat.

She hobbled carefully around the front of the truck, using the hood for support despite its being wet. And wondering just what she was trying to prove.

As she reached the open passenger door, she hesitated. Unable to bear much weight on her bad leg, how was she going to climb up? Nick had helped her on the way here. Darn it, she needed him again.

"You going to yell at me if I help you?"

The wary look on his face surprised her. Had she been that nasty? She tried an apologetic smile. "I'll behave, I promise."

"Stand tight, then." He slid nimbly out of his seat. Seconds later he stood at her side. "Ready?"

She nodded. Warm hands circled her waist. Though she weighed 115 pounds, Nick lifted her as if she were as light as her laptop. She clasped his biceps and felt his muscles flex. So different from Dwight's flabby arms. So very sexy.

"Thank you," she said, her voice not quite steady.

"My pleasure."

Heat flared in his eyes, throwing her body into chaos. He settled her in the bucket seat, his hands lingering a moment on her waist. She wanted him even more than she had this morning. Her hands itched to clasp his neck and pull him close for a kiss. Until she remembered flirty Liz and her suggestive, intimate looks at Nick.

Whatever the two of them had shared, sex likely was included. Hot sex. None of Cinnamon's business, but the very thought put a sour taste in her mouth. "You can let go now," she said coolly.

Jerking as if she'd slapped him, he released her. He shut the door with more force than necessary and headed around the truck to his side. Cinnamon fastened her seat belt with stiff movements.

He climbed into the cab, slamming the door behind him. Before he finished buckling his belt, she spoke.

"I suppose you and Liz date," she said, unable to stem the disapproval in her voice.

"Are you kidding?" Nick shifted out of Park, laughing and shaking his head. "Her son, Bret, is nineteen, only thirteen years younger than I am. She's too old for me, and she's not my type," he stated, glancing straight into Cinnamon's eyes.

Relieved and at the same time feeling foolish, she flushed. "What *is* your type?" She could have bitten her tongue.

As he pulled away from the curb he was still smiling. "A woman who likes to have fun, no strings attached."

"Exactly like Liz," Cinnamon pointed out.

Nick scoffed. "That's all show. She's husband hunting and will do about anything to snag herself one. So far nobody's been fool enough to take the bait." As he waited for several cars to pass, he eyed Cinnamon. "What kind of man do you like?"

"He should be single, upwardly mobile, as I am, financially comfortable and looking to settle down and start a family."

Voicing her requirements aloud reminded her that Nick wasn't what she wanted. Except, he *had* been reading that business magazine in Doc's waiting room, which could mean he was more success-oriented than she'd guessed.

She waited until he turned out of the parking lot to

pose her question. "Did you happen to read the article in *Entrepreneur* about building your business?"

"No," he said. His hands tightened on the wheel and his face closed.

For some reason she'd upset him. Puzzled, she frowned. "Did I somehow offend you?"

"Nope."

Now his whole body was stiff and tense, and a tiny muscle jumped in his jaw.

"Are you sure? Because whatever—"

"Subject closed," he barked, his expression as dark as the cloud-laden sky.

He turned on the radio, cranking up the sound. Country music was not Cinnamon's favorite, especially when it was played so loud the whole truck vibrated. Bracing for an explosion, she cautiously turned down the volume.

None came. Relieved, she sank against the seat. The rest of the drive back, neither she nor Nick spoke. Staring at the modest houses and dripping trees as they sped down the road, Cinnamon mulled over the conversation and tried to figure out what had gone wrong.

Clearly she'd hit a sore spot about Nick's handyman business, though what that could be eluded her. Fran said he was happy with less than full-time work. If he wasn't interested in growing his business, why not just say so? No, she decided, his strong negative reaction stemmed from something more. But what?

She stifled a frustrated sigh. This really wasn't her concern. She had troubles of her own. Still, she *was* curious....

Through lowered lashes she studied Nick. His attention was fixed firmly on the road, his shoulders were taut and his mouth compressed—nonverbal barriers that told her not to broach the subject again.

By the time the sullen man pulled into the Oceanside driveway, Cinnamon could hardly wait to exit the truck and get out of his space, this time without his help.

"Thank you for the ride and your time," she said before opening her door, "and please wish Abby good luck tomorrow."

With his jaw clamped, he gave a terse nod.

Best to stay out of his way the rest of the day. She'd grab something from the fridge and spend the afternoon in her suite, checking e-mails, and if she still didn't hear from her contacts, making calls. Time to search the Internet, too. Plenty to keep her busy.

She wouldn't venture downstairs again until Nick left for the day.

BY MIDAFTERNOON NICK had washed every window and taken paint samples from all rooms and hallways except those in Cinnamon's suite. Since it was nearly time to pick up Abby and Sharon, the suite's windows and overhead fan would have to wait. But first thing

Monday morning he intended to stop at the hardware store for custom-matched paint, so he needed that sample now.

At least, that was what he told himself as he hesitated before Cinnamon's closed door, as uncomfortable as a rebellious kid about to be punished by the school principal.

He lifted his fist to knock but faltered. He and Cinnamon hadn't spoken since the ride home from Doc's this morning. She'd refused his help up the Oceanside steps and had insisted on making her own lunch and taking it upstairs under her own steam.

The awful tension between them had weighted the air, and despite the door separating them, still did. His fault for blowing his cool and holding on to his anger. She'd given him an opportunity to apologize by wishing Abby good luck, yet he'd said nothing.

Nick felt bad about that and about yelling at her—he felt lousy about the whole thing. And wasn't sure he wanted to face her. Maybe he'd get that paint sample Monday, instead.

Coward.

Straightening his shoulders he rapped softly on the door. "Cinnamon? You all right in there?"

"Fine, thank you," came the muffled but chilly reply.

He tried again, fingering the tool belt hanging on his hips. "I need a paint chip to match at the hardware store. Okay if I open the door and come in?"

"Do what you must."

She was nestled in the oversized blue armchair that faced the cloud-darkened view, laptop on her lap and still-bare legs, though she wore socks, propped on the matching ottoman. Rosy lamplight lit the room, and a cheery fire that had been laid by Fran crackled in the fireplace.

A cozy image, except for the bandage on Cinnamon's shin and the pained expression on her face. A result of the injury, or his being here? He stood uncertainly at the threshold while she stared at him. Her expression was cool, but with her head angled a fraction, he knew she expected him to say something.

"How's the leg?" he asked, leaning his shoulder on the doorjamb.

"Bearable, so long as I prop it up."

"Smart, to work stretched out that way," he said, hoping for a smile, or at least a brighter face.

Not a hint of either in sight, only a dismissive shrug. "At the moment I don't feel very smart, but thanks."

"Hey, anybody could have slipped on those wet steps. When I come back on Monday I'll lay nonskid tape on each riser. That should help, and ease Fran's mind. She nearly had a heart attack when I told her what happened to you."

"I spoke with her, too—twice before I convinced her I'm okay." A brief smile flickered and died. "The nonskid tape sounds like a good idea."

She threw a worried glance at the laptop, and he guessed the crack about not feeling smart was more about that than the accident.

"How goes the job search?" he asked.

"Not so well."

A pink flush climbed her face and she looked flustered. Why? "With your background there must be dozens of companies interested in you."

"You'd think. I contacted my friends about that, but they don't seem to want to…" She shook her head, sighed and dropped her gaze. "They won't help me."

"They don't sound like friends to me."

"I thought they were until recently." Frowning, she fussed with the hem of her sweater, smoothing it down. "Guess I was wrong."

That had to sting. "Sorry to hear that."

Up went her chin. She wasn't looking for pity.

"It's nothing I can't deal with. I've been surfing the Web, looking at various consulting company Web sites. Something's bound to come up."

"I'm sure of it."

An awkward silence fell between them, broken only by the crackling fire. Now was a good time for that apology. Nick pushed away from the doorjamb and moved toward her, scrubbing the back of his neck. "Look, I shouldn't have snapped at you this morning."

"No, you shouldn't have. I was only trying to make conversation. I don't even know how I offended you."

Her prickly tone didn't make this easy. "You didn't."

But her question about the magazine article she assumed he'd read had cut too close for comfort. Nobody knew reading was hard for him. Shame burned like acid in his gut, but he didn't let on.

"Oh, no? Then why did you bite my head off and then refuse to talk? If you don't want to build your business, just say so."

The disapproval on her face rankled. Nick hung his thumbs from his belt loops. "I'm comfortable, and the work is mostly steady. Hell, I own my own house. That ought to tell you something."

All right, a three-room cabin and a small, detached workshop, but it was paid for. Though he did need a bundle of cash for Abby's math camp, and Sharon could use some financial help... None of that was Cinnamon's concern. Nick narrowed his eyes and crossed his arms. "Just why are you so interested my life?"

"I'm not," she said, slapping shut the laptop. "I'm simply finishing this morning's conversation."

"Well, it was too damned nosy for me. I'm not one of your clients, and I don't need your help." His temper was climbing again, and with effort he reined it in. Cinnamon's mouth opened, but he cut her off. "Why'd you let me think you were fired from your job, when you quit?"

Her turn to tense up. "Resigned," she corrected. Though her expression remained calm, her back went soldier straight. "What exactly did Fran tell you?"

"Nothing. That's why I'm asking. Isn't it better to quit than get fired?"

Her hands started their fidgety routine, rubbing circles over the closed laptop. "That depends."

"On what?" he asked, genuinely wanting to know.

"The problem was…personal."

"What'd you do, tell the boss to shove it?"

She laughed without humor. "Not exactly. I…well, it's not a story I want to share. It's private."

"And my business isn't?"

Comprehension dawned, and she almost smiled. "Touché." She settled into her chair again, looking far more relaxed.

Relieved that the tension between them had eased, Nick turned to go.

"Nick? Don't forget to wish Abby good luck from me."

This was the second time she'd offered good wishes and the first time Nick had smiled. "Thanks. I will."

Whistling, he left.

It was only on the drive home that he realized he'd forgotten to get a paint chip from Cinnamon's suite. He shook his head, wondering at his forgetfulness and not pleased that she affected him so strongly.

In so many ways they were wrong for each other. He knew that in his head, yet when he was near her, reason and logic seemed to fade.

Good thing he was headed out of town for a few days, because he needed to get his mind off the woman. He wouldn't think about her all weekend, he pledged.

Surely by Monday, she'd be out of his system.

Chapter Seven

Whistling softly to the Dixie Chicks song Sharon had inserted in the tape player, Nick drove down the winding, two-lane road that would eventually lead to the freeway and Portland. Though it was nearly five o'clock and rush hour, traffic was light. But then in the off season in rural Oregon, it generally was.

He could have made better time, but Sharon's old wagon didn't have the pep of his truck. What it did have was a back seat with seat belts. After a long, hard week, Nick's sister had readily agreed that he should drive the four hours to Portland and that Abby should sit up front. Now, head cushioned by a pillow, Sharon slept soundly in the back. While in the passenger seat up front, his niece was as quiet and still as her mother, but not asleep. Nervous, Nick guessed, but in the early darkness of winter he couldn't quite make out her expression.

"How're you doing?" he asked softly so as not to disturb Sharon.

"Why didn't you and Mom tell me?" Voice low, Abby sent him a withering look he felt more than saw.

"Tell you what?"

"That the Cranberry Factory might close. You should have told me!"

Her voice was loud now. And here he'd thought her solemn air had been due to tomorrow's math bee. Praying Sharon was awake now, because he sure as hell didn't want to deal with the scary subject alone, Nick shot a hopeful glance in the rearview mirror. Still out cold. He was on his own.

"Where'd you hear that?" he asked, buying time so he could figure out what to say.

"Everybody at school's talking about it."

"Well, at this point, it's only a rumor," he assured her. Which was mostly true.

"I don't care," Abby accused. "I have the right to know."

"You've been working so hard to prepare for the math bee, and we didn't want you to lose your focus. Face it, kid, you're a worrier."

"That's a lame reason! I'm not a baby anymore, so quit treating me like one!"

Her dramatic tone was almost comical, but her hurt feelings and the possible factory closure were nothing to joke about. "Think we don't know you're growing up? I swear we'd have told you if there was anything to tell."

By her arms crossed over her chest and her loud, angry huff, he could see the kid wasn't buying what he said.

"There's a town meeting about the situation next Tuesday night, and—"

"What's going on up there?" Sharon called sleepily from the back.

"We're talking about the factory," Nick said, shooting a help-me look at the rearview mirror.

"And that you hid your problems from me. I'm coming with you to that town meeting," Abby insisted. "That way, I'll know the same stuff you know."

Sometimes his niece was too damn smart for her own good. "Brother," Nick muttered.

"Now that she knows, she *should* come," Sharon said. "Don't you think, Nick?"

Why not? Abby was dead-on—she had the right to know. He shrugged his agreement.

Satisfied, the girl nodded and uncrossed her arms.

A sign pointed to the upcoming freeway entrance. Nick glanced at her again. "You hungry, kid? 'Cause once we get on the freeway it's another two hours to Portland. This is a good time to stop for dinner, get gas and stretch your legs."

"I'm not eating tonight," she announced.

Since she was at the age when she was always hungry, this surprised him. "What?"

"Well, I am," Sharon said. "I'm starved."

Abby glanced over her shoulder at her mother. "We should have brought sandwiches to save money."

So that was the deal. He sighed. "This is exactly why we didn't tell you about the factory."

Leaning forward, Sharon nodded. "Stewing over what hasn't even happened yet won't do any good, and certainly won't help you win the math bee."

"Your brain needs nourishment, both tonight and in the morning," Nick added, because that kind of logic usually worked on Abby.

"I'm not sure I want to win anymore," she mumbled in a voice so low he was sure he'd misunderstood.

He frowned. "Say what?"

"If Mom loses her job, how will we pay for my room and board at math camp?"

Sharon didn't offer any answers, and Nick knew she was fretting about the same thing. Not that she could pay those costs even if she kept her job. The bulk of that expense weighed on his shoulders.

"You leave that to us, okay? We'll get you there," he assured her, hoping he was right.

Maybe Cinnamon was on to something—he needed to boost his business, and fast. He thought about asking her for advice, but his pride wouldn't let him. Besides, she might expect him to read that article, a chore that could take decades. He'd always managed on his own. He'd figure this out for himself. And he wasn't going to think about Cinnamon this weekend.

Yet he couldn't help wondering about the so-called friends who couldn't or wouldn't help her find a job. And why in the world had she resigned from what had to be a high-salary position?

Not his business, and he had enough problems without worrying about her. But here he was, doing it anyway, wishing he could hold her and ease her troubles with kisses and more....

As his body stirred to life, Abby released a heavy sigh.

"Okay, I'll eat, but only if we go someplace cheap."

"You got it, kid." Crisis averted.

"I see a fast-food place on the left ahead," Sharon said. "And a gas station on the same side of the street."

"How lucky can you get?" Slowing, Nick signaled and pushed Cinnamon from his thoughts.

JUST BEFORE NOON ON Friday, Rosy set a throw pillow on a café chair and frowned as Cinnamon gingerly propped up her leg. "How does that feel, hon?"

"The pillow helps," Cinnamon replied, touched by the restaurant owner's attention and concern. "Thanks."

"Because if it still hurts, I could bring you a glass of whiskey...." Rosy's eyes widened comically.

Cinnamon laughed and shook her head. "No thanks."

"At last, she smiles," Rosy quipped to Fran, who sat beside Cinnamon. "That's what I wanted to see.

I'll be back with coffee—unspiked." She winked. "Sorry, Cinnamon, you had your chance."

The gentle teasing made Cinnamon feel liked, a welcome change from the rejection by her business "friends." Between their hurtful snubbing and her sore shin she hadn't slept well. Stretching her arms overhead, she yawned.

Earning her a concerned frown from Fran. "Sure you're up to meeting the Friday Girls?" She glanced at the five empty chairs around the table, soon to be filled with the women she lunched with every Friday from late October through early May. "Of course, we did reserve this table. Wouldn't want to disappoint Rosy."

Judging by the sparse number of diners, that was likely true. Friday lunch business was slow, which was to be expected in early February.

"Wouldn't want to disappoint Rosy," Cinnamon echoed. "Besides, I can't wait to meet the friends I've heard about forever. And you made a special trip back to the Oceanside to pick me up for this." She glanced at her shin. "Since you won't let me drive."

"It won't hurt you to rely on other people for transportation for a day or two."

"Except that after lunch, you're stuck driving me back again."

"Happy to do it. I just wish I could spend the rest of the afternoon with you," Fran admitted guiltily. "But with the Valentine's Day dance in two weeks and the Love on Main Street outdoor art show coinciding…" She shook her head. "Since I'm heading up the entertainment committee, I'm stuck."

"Hey, I'm a big girl," Cinnamon said. "I don't need you to babysit me."

Though without Fran, the Oceanside seemed awfully big and way too quiet. Too bad Nick was in Portland….

The moment she thought of him, she frowned. Hadn't she already wasted far too much time fixated on the man? During brief snatches of sleep last night she'd even dreamed about him. Vivid, erotic stuff of them in bed, doing all sorts of fun and deliciously naughty things, unfortunately without any sexual release…. The private places in her body clenched in frustration, and heat rushed to her face.

"Are you too warm?" Fran asked.

Rather than answer that, Cinnamon changed the subject. "What exactly is the Love on Main Street outdoor art show, and isn't this a risky time of year to display art outside?"

"Actually, we put up a giant, open-sided tent in the town hall parking lot, with heaters inside," Fran explained. "The carvings, sculptures, drawings and paintings are done by locals and must depict love in some way—of the sea, the beach, Cranberry, lovers, pets and so forth. We all have a great time. Too bad you'll be gone by then."

Not only gone, but hopefully about to start a new job. Cinnamon truly wanted that. And yet… "I'm sorry I'll miss that," she replied wistfully.

"Some other time. Did you have better luck with this morning's job search?"

Cinnamon shook her head. "I called a few more colleagues who hadn't replied to my e-mails, but they brushed me off the same as everyone else. 'You know how conservative consulting companies are.'" She mimicked in a sarcastic tone the rationale she'd heard over and over. Which was absolutely true. And the consulting world was a tight-knit community, making it tough to break into and, if you got into trouble, rough to change jobs.

"Not one of them cared about Dwight's promises to me or what really happened between us." In their view she was a home wrecker and a woman willing to do anything, including seduce the boss, to climb the corporate ladder. Not that any of them was brave enough to say so. To a person, they mouthed polite excuses and hung up as quickly as possible.

For a moment anger and disappointment threatened to ruin her appetite, but Cinnamon refused to let her negative feelings get the best of her or ruin today's lunch. "Their loss," she said in what she hoped was a confident voice.

"Absolutely," Fran seconded. "If you ask me, your colleagues are a bunch of lame-brains." Her eyes flashed indignation. "It isn't right to discount your considerable skills and experience simply because your relationship with the boss went sour. Especially when you've proved yourself over and over again."

"We're on the same page there. Though, looking back, I could have used better judgment." Cinnamon shook her head. "I was a naive fool."

"If you learned something from the experience," her friend said, "it wasn't all for naught."

"I guess not," Cinnamon said, though she wasn't certain just what she had learned. Fran looked worried, so Cinnamon gave her a reassuring smile. "Don't worry, I'll find my way. I always have."

I just hope I find work before my savings run out. Her insides trembled at the thought.

"Tough, feisty and determined." Her friend nodded approvingly. "There's the Cinnamon I know and love."

"That's me, all right." Cinnamon straightened her shoulders and shifted in her seat, which jostled her leg. She winced.

"On top of your job worries, you go and get hurt." Fran squeezed her hand. "I'm sorry about the accident."

"It's not your fault I fell."

"Since you slipped on my wet steps, I'm afraid it's very much my responsibility. If you sue me…well, I'll understand."

Cinnamon's jaw dropped. "You know darn well I'd never do that. I'm better today than yesterday, and in a day or two I'll be good as new. Be glad it was me who fell, and not someone else."

"I'd rather *no* one get hurt. Good thing Nick can fix the problem. He promised to pick up some of that nonstick tape first thing Monday morning and put a strip on every step—provided the weather cooperates." Fran glanced out the large picture window fronting the street, where a sleeting rain much like yesterday's pummeled the glass. "For safety's sake, let's hope for a sunny Monday."

There she went, mentioning Nick, and just when Cinnamon had managed to get him out of her brain.

Steaming coffeepot in hand, Rosy hastened over and deftly filled two mugs. "Speaking of Nick," she said, picking up the conversation as if she'd been at the table all along, "any word on how Abby did at that math bee this morning?"

Fran shook her head. "We probably won't hear until after they get back. If they get back too late tonight, and I suspect they will, it'll be tomorrow."

"Well, call me if you hear anything," Rosy said.

Fran nodded. "You do the same. I think I'll run to the ladies' room now, before everyone arrives," she said as the waitress bustled off. "Be right back."

Cinnamon nodded absently, her thoughts on Nick and his bubbly niece. Had the girl won the math competition? Since she wanted the win so badly and her mother and uncle fully supported her, Cinnamon hoped so.

More pressing and worrisome, why did she continue to think and dream about Nick when he had no drive and no ambition to move up in life? She wanted a man who valued the things she did, not the sweet, attractive handyman who caused mental confusion and heart palpitations. She sighed. Face it, she was in lust, big-time, and no amount of self-talk could fix that.

If only he hadn't come to her room yesterday afternoon, his expression wary, arms crossed over his shirt, and long legs planted before her, with that sexy tool belt hanging low on his narrow hips. After the accident and the brush-off by her colleagues, she'd been upset and vulnerable, and prepared to stay mad at him for snapping at her earlier.

But his sincere apology, warm eyes and full attention had weakened her resolve and made her want to trust him. She'd actually considered talking about Dwight. Luckily she'd come to her senses, for if Nick knew about that, he might think the same low things about her that other people did.

But he didn't know, and with her so-called friends shutting her out, his interest and kindness drew her to him like a dry sponge to water. No wonder she'd had those dreams.

"I'm back." Fran slid into her seat. "I wonder where—"

Suddenly the door opened and a group of women trouped in. "There they are." She smiled and waved.

Five hands waved in return. The women hung their coats on the coat tree. Then, chattering as if they hadn't seen each other in years, they headed for the table. One by one they introduced themselves to Cinnamon, each expressing sympathy over her injury.

Betsy—at thirty, the same age as Cinnamon and Fran—was married with grade-schoolers and owned a yarn shop. Lynn, divorced and the town's postmistress, and Claire, who owned and ran the dry cleaner's, were about ten years older. Joelle and Noelle, never-married fraternal twins and retired bed-and-breakfast owners, were well past seventy.

Talking and laughing and smelling of damp, fresh air, they arranged themselves around the table, Betsy beside Cinnamon, and Joelle and Noelle directly across from her.

They seemed as colorful and as much fun as Fran had said. Cinnamon brightened, certain that at last she could banish Nick from her thoughts.

"FRAN SAYS YOU LIKE to shop," Betsy commented as she finished a piece of Rosy's coconut cream pie.

Cinnamon liked the woman, who seemed keenly intelligent with a ready sense of humor. "I do, but since I'm unemployed, I'll stick to browsing," she replied, surprised that she was able to joke about her predicament.

Betsy shrugged. "Browsing works for me. It's been a real slow morning, so before lunch I closed up shop for the rest of the day. The kids don't get home from school till three-forty-five, and I have two free hours ahead. Why don't I show you some of our shops? I'll even reopen mine, if you want." She glanced at Cinnamon's leg. "That is, if you feel up to it. Either way, I'll drive you to Fran's."

Not about to give in to her injury, Cinnamon nodded. "Sounds fun. And your driving will save her an extra trip home. I'd love to see your shop. Though I can't help but wonder how many people around here knit."

"You'd be surprised," Betsy said. "Tourists buy yarn, too."

"Can we stop at the Cranberries-to-Go shop, too?" Cinnamon said. "I met the owner, Liz, at the doctor's office yesterday and said I would."

"Did you?" Her new friend's eyes widened speculatively. "I'll bet she didn't appreciate seeing Nick with you. Was she nasty?"

Cinnamon recalled the tall, buxom blonde who had introduced herself. "No, she was friendly and warm. Probably because there's nothing between Nick and me."

Every woman at the table was listening with

clear interest, so she spoke to them all. "We're hardly even friends."

"But Nick drove you to Doc's. Then he stayed and waited for you," Betsy pointed out.

"So? If Liz had hurt her leg, I'm sure he'd have done the same."

"Maybe, maybe not," replied Lynn, the postmistress who sat on Betsy's other side. An intent expression brightened her weathered face as she leaned around Betsy to catch Cinnamon's eye. "See, Liz has a thing for Nick. She's always been wild for him."

Claire, who sat opposite Lynn, nodded. "Tell her about that time at the post office, Claire."

"You mean when they both showed up at the same time, and Liz did everything possible to seduce the man?" She shook her head in disgust, her short, gray bob swaying. "Rubbing her chest and licking her lips in broad daylight, not caring who saw her. Shameless! It's a good thing no other customers were around. Nick ignored her, bless his heart."

"Can you imagine?" Claire tsked. "That woman is way too hungry for male attention."

Lynn gave a knowing nod. "It scares men off."

"She got pregnant and married while she was still in high school," Betsy said. "But the marriage didn't last. Her ex moved away, leaving her when Bret was just a baby."

"A real tough situation," Joelle sympathized. "But you gotta hand it to her because she did—"

"—get her GED." Noelle nodded. "And worked her way from a clerk—"

"—to owner of Cranberries-to-Go," Joelle finished for her twin.

"That's admirable," Cinnamon said. "Nick says she's looking for a man to settle down with."

"That can't be true." Claire looked surprised. "She's been divorced nearly twenty years and loves to flirt. Wonder where he got that idea?"

"Maybe she proposed," Joelle said.

The entire table laughed.

"All I know is he doesn't want to settle down," Cinnamon said. "You know, Liz's son is nine-teen, only thirteen years younger than Nick," she added, quoting his very words. "She's too old for him."

Inwardly she frowned. Want to or not, here she was, thinking and talking about Nick. Again.

Joelle and Noelle offered matching sage nods. "Plenty of ladies besides Liz have tried to catch him," Joelle said. "But he's never dated the same woman for long. I—"

"—wonder why that is?" Noelle posited.

"What do you think, Cinnamon?" the twins asked in unison.

The question drew the interest of everyone at the

table including Rosy, who was stacking dirty plates onto a tray.

"I wouldn't know."

Fran shot her a sly, sideways glance. "My guess is, he hasn't met the right person."

Talking about Nick made Cinnamon uncomfortable, especially with six women eyeing her. She focused on Fran. "Shouldn't you be getting to your meeting?"

Fran hastily looked at her watch. "I almost forgot!" Grabbing her purse, she jumped up, setting off a chain reaction.

"Good to meet you all," Cinnamon said.

"You're a lovely young woman." Joelle smiled. "We must do this again—"

"—before you leave town." Noelle patted her blue-gray perm. "How about next Friday?"

"Sure you want to go in there?" Betsy nodded at the metal Cranberries-to-Go sign hanging over the door.

Cinnamon and she had spent the last hour touring the shops, and when her leg hurt, sitting and talking like old friends. She felt nearly as comfortable with Betsy as she did with Fran.

Oddly, she'd never felt this relaxed around her colleagues. No wonder they didn't treat her like a friend— they'd never been more than business associates.

The insight was a disturbing one, and she wondered at herself. She'd been so wrapped up in work that she'd mistaken acquaintances for something more. How pathetic.

She peered through the window, glimpsing jars, kitchenware and oven mitts emblazoned with cranberries. "Looks interesting to me. And I did tell Liz I'd stop by." Noting Betsy's round eyes and curious expression, she frowned. "What?"

"I just thought, given that she's been after Nick all these years, and given that he was with you at Doc's…"

Cinnamon groaned. "We went over this at lunch, remember?" She shook her head at the cloud-laden sky. "There's nothing between Nick and me. He's not my type." Moving as fast as her injury allowed, she opened the door and limped through it.

"All right, but don't say I didn't warn you," Betsy murmured, following her inside.

Save for Liz, the small store was empty.

"Hello there." Her carefully made-up face brightened. "You're my first customer in ages. I was just about to close up shop."

"I locked up at noon," Betsy said.

Brow creased, Liz glanced from Cinnamon to Betsy. "You two know each other?"

"We met today at lunch."

"That Friday girls thing Fran started, huh?"

Apparently everybody in town knew about the weekly get-together. Which wasn't surprising.

"I can't buy anything today," Cinnamon said. "But I wanted to see your shop."

"That's okay. How's your leg? Does it still hurt?"

"I think I'll live, thanks."

Liz arched one penciled brow toward Betsy. "How's that darling husband of yours?" She smiled at Cinnamon. "Cal's my CPA, and I just adore the man."

"You adore every man," Betsy muttered.

If Liz heard, she didn't let on. "Any news on Abby?" she asked Cinnamon.

"Not that I've heard."

"I thought for sure Nick would have called you by now."

Betsy regarded Cinnamon with an I-told-you-so smirk.

Cinnamon frowned. "Why would he do that?"

"I saw how he looked at you in Doc's office, and I figured…" She winked. "You know."

What was this, a conspiracy? "You figured wrong," Cinnamon said for what seemed the dozenth time. "Nick brought me to Doc's because he had to. We're not involved, and he doesn't have feelings for me."

"Think what you want, but I've known him for years. He's never looked at *me* that way." Liz leaned toward Betsy. "Like he wanted to eat her for lunch." She fanned her red-tipped talons and blew on them, while Cinnamon's cheeks warmed and Betsy grinned.

"If he just once looked at me like that, I'd be head-over-heels and halfway to heaven."

Cinnamon *had* seen Nick's eyes go dark and feverish when he looked at her. Her insides warmed and tingled, and she knew exactly what Liz meant. "You're imagining things," she lied. "Even if I wanted to get involved with Nick, which I don't, there's no time for that. A week from Monday I'll be headed back to L.A."

For what, she didn't know. Not a job...yet.

Liz's mouth pursed in a coy expression. "That's enough time for an affair."

Betsy nodded. "She's right."

Cinnamon gaped at the woman she'd spent the past few hours with, wondering whether she knew her at all. She hadn't told her about Dwight, but they *had* discussed relationships and men in general.

"I don't do those," she stated.

Liz smiled. "Maybe you should."

Just then Betsy's cell phone rang. "Excuse me," she said, slipping it from her shoulder bag.

Tired of the conversation, Cinnamon stared past Liz. "Think I'll look around now."

"Enjoy."

Cinnamon wandered past shelves of cranberry chutney, sugared cranberries and cranberry cosmetics. She picked up a porcelain plate decorated with cranberries and absently noted the full set of matching pieces, all the while musing over Liz's suggestion.

Have a quickie affair with Nick?

She certainly lusted after him enough for that, and she definitely was over Dwight. But affairs were something her mother did, over and over. Not Cinnamon. She had committed sex—it didn't happen outside serious relationships headed toward forever. With successful men, or those on their way up the corporate ladder. None had lasted, but that was just bad luck, relationships gone sour. Not affairs.

She stopped at a table of silky bikini panties emblazoned with cranberries and sifted through them for her size. What about Dwight? Even though she'd thought that eventually they would get married, in the end what they'd shared was just a tawdry affair that had cost her the job she loved, and ruined her career.

No, affairs caused nothing but heartache and trouble. Even so, making love with Nick was a definite temptation.

Appalled, Cinnamon dropped the panties and turned away. No more of that. Pulling a cranberry cookbook from a display, she leafed through it with pretended interest. She would not have an affair with Nick, and why in the world had Liz put the idea in her head? Never mind. In ten days she'd leave. Until then she'd simply close off her emotions as she had at Sabin and Howe.

Compared to weeks spent stifling her feelings there, ten days was nothing.

Chapter Eight

Monday morning dawned clear and crisp. Rested and pleased at Abby's success, nonskid tape and tools in hand, Nick whistled as he strode across Fran's veranda. He carefully avoided thoughts of Cinnamon. Out of sight, out of mind had worked well for him, and whether or not he saw her today, he intended to keep himself occupied by work.

With a long of list of chores, that shouldn't be hard. He strode through the dining room sliders in search of coffee and nearly plowed into Cinnamon.

"Whoa. You're in a big hurry," he said, looking her over.

Coat on, keys in hand, she looked to be on her way out. Her eyes were bright and her skin glowed with good health. She was more beautiful than ever.

"Um, thanks."

Her cheeks flushed the way he liked and her gaze

darted away and he realized he'd spoken out loud. His turn to go hot-faced.

Yet he couldn't look away. It had only been two days, but he couldn't believe how good it was to see her. Or how much he wanted her.

So much for getting her out of his system.

He set down his tools and supplies. "Where are you off to?"

"Meeting Betsy Grand for coffee," she replied in a crisp voice he'd never heard.

She seemed aloof and not interested in making conversation. Which should have been a relief, but wasn't.

Nick scratched the back of his neck. After apologizing Friday, he'd assumed they'd cleared the air. Looked as if he'd thought wrong. Better off with her being distant. Maybe he should leave things alone.

"If you're going out and wearing those pretty beige slacks, your leg must be better," he said instead.

"Much, thanks."

"That's good news."

"I hear you have good news, too. How wonderful that Abby took first place in the state for her age category. You and Sharon must be so proud."

"We are." His chest puffed as he grinned. "Abby's over the moon."

"Please congratulate her for me."

He nodded.

Silence.

Not quite ready to let her go, Nick searched his mind for something to say. "I'll be doing paint touch-ups today," he said at last. "I still need a sample from the Orca Suite to match at the hardware store. Okay if I get that this morning?"

"Certainly."

Refusing to meet his eye, she stared at his shoulder and fiddled with her keys, their jingling the only sound in the room. Every clink upped the tension between them.

"I'm trying like hell to make conversation, and you're stiff as a corpse," he said. "Are you still upset about Thursday, or did I do something else to make you mad?"

Abruptly the jangling stopped. "It's not you," she answered, sounding more like the Cinnamon he knew and liked. But she still wouldn't look at him.

He waited for her to explain, but she didn't. So he pushed. "What is it, then?"

Her lips compressed, and she shook her head.

"Fine," he snapped, seriously irritated. "You want to be in a foul mood, suit yourself." Wheeling away, he strode into the kitchen, snatched up the mug Fran had left by the coffeemaker and filled it.

"Where's Fran?" he asked, sounding gruff even to his own ears.

Cinnamon shot a nervous glance at the door. "Picking up a gift for Abby. Something from both of us."

That last part surprised him so much he nearly snorted his coffee. "You only met her once."

"That was enough to know I like her. I admire her, too, and I'm very proud of what she accomplished." The guarded expression vanished, and at last she met his eyes.

Nick didn't understand the sudden change in her mood, but under her warm, direct look and words his temper faded. "You should have seen her, Cinnamon. She was calm and cool. With all the stress of competing, I never thought she'd be able to relax as much as she did. Watching her up there was amazing." He shook his head in wonder. "Where she got those smarts, I don't know. Not from our side of the family."

"You're no dummy, Nick."

She wouldn't say that if she knew he barely could read. Dropping his gaze to the dark liquid in his mug, he shrugged. "Anyway, you'd have enjoyed watching her."

"I wish I'd been there."

Damned if she didn't sound and look as if she meant that. "So do I," he said, staring at her generous mouth.

"Did she use your breathing technique?"

"Yep. Anytime you want me to teach it to you, I will." His offer surprised him, but then, he was talking out of desire.

What in the world had made him think he could forget about wanting her? One friendly glance and he was gone.

"I'll think about it."

Her lips parted a fraction, the bottom lip full and tempting. Drawn by a force he couldn't fight and hardly aware of what he was doing, he set down his mug and moved toward her.

Cinnamon swallowed. "Wh-what prize did she win?"

Her expression posed a different question that had nothing to do with Abby and everything to do with Nick.

She wanted him.

The knowledge aroused him more than any fantasy. He was so focused on her eyes and mouth and so hot for her, he barely heard the question. He tried to speak, but his throat was dry. Clearing it, he tried again. "Two weeks at an elite math camp this summer, tuition paid."

He'd saved enough for the required deposit on her room and board. The rest he'd earn if he had to work day and night, seven days a week.

"How wonderful for her." Her eyes darkened, and the need he saw there burned into his very soul.

God, he wanted to kiss her. He stuffed his hands into the pockets of his jeans. "It'll give her a good start toward getting into college."

"Yes," she breathed, as if she'd heard his thoughts.

She was impossible to resist. Giving in to his fierce hunger to touch her, he cupped her chin. Her skin was smooth and soft and warm, and beneath his palm her pulse jumped wildly.

"You mean that?"

"I don't know what you're talking about," she whispered, but her yearning look told him otherwise.

"See, I have this big problem," he confessed, staring into her eyes. "I'm attracted to you, but I don't want to be."

"I understand completely. That's why I was cool a little while ago—trying to keep my distance." She gave her head a slow shake. "We're not right for each other."

"Yet here we are." Stroking her jawline with his thumbs, he coaxed her face up.

Her eyelids dropped a fraction, the thick, dark lashes seductively lowered.

Blood pounded in his veins. "You don't know how much I want to kiss you right now."

"I think I do." She pulled in a shuddering breath. "What should we do about that?"

"The only thing we can do—get this over with so we can put it behind us and move on."

The keys dropped from her fingers.

"You think that will work?" she asked, searching his gaze.

"Whether it does or not, I'm going to kiss you."

CINNAMON KNEW SHE should stop Nick before it was too late, but she needed his kiss the way she needed air. Every nerve and muscle in her body primed and aching, she closed her eyes and offered her mouth. It seemed like forever before his lips at last touched hers, tentative and soft, a teasing brush of flesh against flesh. And again.

She didn't want teasing. She wanted passion. Now.

"That's no kiss," she whispered against his mouth.

Impatient and suddenly ravenous, she threaded her fingers through his thick black hair as she'd longed to do for days, and pulled him closer. Somehow her coat had come off, bringing them into more intimate contact. Standing on her toes, sore shin forgotten, she planted a fevered kiss on his lips.

"Very nice," he murmured hoarsely, "but not enough."

His arms wrapped around her and anchored her tight against his hard body. "Open your mouth."

She did. He slanted his head and slipped his tongue inside. This kiss was hotter than she'd ever imagined or experienced.

She tasted coffee. And lost herself in a haze of sensation—the taut strength of Nick's arms, the solid warmth of his body, the enticing scent of pine soap and man. Heart pounding, she breathed his breath and shared hers in turn. Moisture pooled between her legs, along with a deep, needy ache. She hooked the calf of her injured leg behind his knee and wriggled against the rigid flesh of his desire.

A growl rumbled his chest. He slid his hand to her aching breast, cupped her and squeezed gently. Dear heaven, she was fast melting beyond the point of no return. With very little effort she would climax.

The force of her need scared her. Nick was wrong for her. This was wrong!

"Nick." She unhooked her leg and pulled back. "We can't do this."

Groaning he released her, his eyes fevered and his breathing ragged. He glanced at the bulge straining against his zipper and offered a humorless smile. "Looks as if this experiment failed."

Cinnamon stared at the proof of his desire. No amount of logic could erase her longing for release, both for herself and Nick. That terrified her. To keep from reaching out to him, she scooped up her coat and keys. "I…I have to go now."

She whirled away and hurried through the sliding door.

EARLY TUESDAY AFTERNOON Fran ushered the mayor and the other three town council members into the small conference room inside the town hall building. In a bold-faced lie she'd told Cinnamon she was at yet another Valentine's Day planning committee. Now, feeling sneaky but good about what she was about to propose, she closed the door firmly behind her and joined the others at the oval table.

They stared expectantly at her, four forty-something professionals who worked at demanding, full-time jobs while also setting the town budget and creating the policies that helped Cranberry run smoothly.

"I appreciate your taking time from your jobs," Fran said. "I know you're wondering why I called this emergency conference when I'm not even on the council, so I'll get right to the point." She looked at each person in turn, noting their curious expressions. "The cranberry factory is about to go under and we have got to do something about that."

"That's why we're holding a town hall meeting to-night." Mayor Eric Jannings, who owned Jannings Real Estate, folded his meaty hands on the table. Great furrows appeared in his fleshy forehead. "Why call a secret, emergency meeting now?"

Anne Trueblood and her law partner, Pete Sperry, looked equally puzzled, and Chet Avery, principal of Cranberry Grade and High School, raised his rust-colored brows in question.

"Because I think I know a way to save our factory."

All four council members leaned forward intently.

"You all know my friend Cinnamon Smith is visit-ing from L.A."

Chet nodded. "Abby Mahoney mentioned that. She

says Miss Smith is real nice, and that you and she gave her a gift certificate for winning the math bee."

"She prefers to be called Cinnamon, and she is wonderful," Fran said. "At the moment she's also an unemployed consultant. Her expertise just happens to be helping companies on the verge of bankruptcy. She's saved dozens, some in worse shape than Tate's. She toured the place and talked with some of the people who work there, so she knows what's going on." She paused, then delivered the idea that had broadsided her a few hours earlier. "I think we ought to recruit her to save it."

During the thoughtful silence that followed, the mayor rubbed his chin pensively. Chet pondered the matter while rubbing the space between his brows, Pete scribbled on the yellow pad he'd brought along and Anne frowned at the table while absently smoothing the chignon at her nape.

"She probably charges an arm and a leg," Anne said at last.

The mayor nodded. "I was thinking the same thing. We don't have the money."

"I know," Fran said, aiming a look at the mayor. "That's where you come in. You have clout, and Tate might listen to you. You could call him and convince him to hire her."

"I can ask," Mayor Jannings said with a doubtful frown. "But Tate's a tough nut."

"Hell, Eric, you're the best salesman in town.

You could sell a cranberry bog to a person looking for vacation property," Pete enthused, a look of pure admiration on his overworked face. "Don't ask the man, *sell* him."

After a thoughtful silence, the mayor straightened his shoulders, the movement causing his blue sports coat to strain across his bulky shoulders. He nodded. "Will do."

"Great," Fran said. "Because Cinnamon will be at tonight's meeting. If we could start off with the good news that Tate's hired her, people will leave feeling hopeful." Including Cinnamon, who'd seemed unusually glum and edgy last night and this morning, no doubt over worry about her lack of job prospects.

Anne nodded. "Heaven knows, we could all use a dose of optimism."

"Good plan," Chet said approvingly. "But even great salespeople fail sometimes. What if Eric *doesn't* convince Tate to hire her?"

The mayor's fingers tapped rapidly on the tabletop. "Then we'd better have plan D ready." He glanced around the table. "Suggestions, anyone?"

"Isn't that why we called tonight's meeting?" Anne asked. "For ideas on how to save the factory?"

"We're bound to get some worth pursuing," Pete said. "Still, we should each come with one or two."

Fran shrugged. "Even if Tate doesn't want to hire Cinnamon, we can ask her for advice."

"Let's hope she has some," the mayor said.

Chapter Nine

Tuesday night Cinnamon and Fran entered the town hall well in advance of the meeting, behind a throng of worried, chattering citizens.

"There's a huge crowd here," she commented over the buzz of conversation vibrating through the spacious room. "Are you sure I should take up a seat?"

Fran gave her a don't-be-silly look. "Of course. I want you to see how our town works and meet the mayor and city council members. And on the selfish side, this is a way to spend time with you."

"You've convinced me," Cinnamon said. Only six days left before she headed back to L.A. to do…who knew what. No job offers had come through, which was unsettling, to say the least. The familiar fear knotted her stomach, but she didn't want to deal with that tonight. She forced a smile. "Thank you again for letting me visit."

Fran looked guilty. "I know I've said this before, but I'm truly sorry I haven't spent more time with you."

"And I've told you a dozen times, I'm fine by myself. At least over the last eight days we've seen each other more than in the past five years. Any time spent together is something to be thankful for."

Two men and a woman dressed in business suits waved and started forward. Fran waved back. "There are three of the town council members I'd like you to meet. Come on."

Cinnamon pushed through the sea of people, recognizing a number of familiar faces. Men and women greeted her with smiles. She exchanged hellos with Bill Patterson and Doc, who asked about her much-improved shin. She noticed Liz, who was busy with two somber-faced male companions and didn't see her.

"Look at Liz," she commented to Fran. "A teenage boy on one arm and a man on the other. Neither one looks happy about that."

"Those are her son, Bret, and her brother, Andy."

Cinnamon's jaw dropped, and Fran chuckled at her obvious surprise before she sobered. "Both work at the cranberry factory, so you can understand why they're worried. Look, there are Joelle and Noelle." Cinnamon and Fran waved.

She greeted Rosy and Claire and Betsy, and met Betsy's husband and adorable young son and daughter.

So many friends. She almost felt as if she belonged here. At the thought, Cinnamon gave her head a mental shake. She was no small-town girl. She loved the energy that pulsed through big cities and all the amenities urban life offered. But amenities and hustle-bustle couldn't compensate for the warmth of the people in Cranberry. *I could never live here,* she silently argued, puzzled that she would even entertain such thoughts. *There are no job opportunities and no available men with the qualifications I want.*

Certainly not Nick. Hardly aware of her actions, she glanced around, searching for him and his family, but not finding them.

Would she see him?

After what happened yesterday she hoped not.

Those kisses had ignited passions she still didn't understand and had blown her plan to wall off her emotions straight to hell. The very memory of kissing Nick set her body humming, the familiar hunger stirring low in her belly.

Oh, could he kiss. He was probably a fantastic lover, too. But she wasn't going to find out about that. Lust after him or not, she couldn't handle a quick fling.

After those kisses, she'd stayed away from the Oceanside the rest of the day, spending time with Betsy, who miraculously hadn't asked any probing questions. Then she'd driven aimlessly through the winding hills surrounding Cranberry, the dark sky and endless rain suiting her mood. Later she'd holed up in the town library, using their computer to search out information on various consulting firms.

She'd returned to the Oceanside after five, when Nick was sure to be gone. Today he'd stayed away, claiming work elsewhere, which was a huge relief. Because the only safe thing to do was to avoid him.

Yet even as she reminded herself, she craned her neck, searching for him. Catching herself, she frowned. If she were smart she'd change her plans and leave tomorrow.

"Here they come," Fran said, indicating the council members. "Let's save seats for ourselves." Indicating two folding chairs in the front row, center, she slipped out of her jacket. "Give me your coat."

As she tossed both wraps on seats, the council members reached them.

"Great crowd, huh?" Fran said over the noise. "Cinnamon, meet Anne Trueblood and Pete Sperry, law partners, and our school principal, Chet Avery."

The three council members shook hands with Cinnamon and welcomed her.

"You must be proud of Abby Mahoney," she said to Chet.

His face lit up and he nodded with enthusiasm. "She's a talented student, indeed."

"The entire town is thrilled," Anne said. "Fran

probably told you about plans to salute Abby at next week's Valentine's Day dinner and dance. I hope you'll be there."

Cinnamon thought again about the warm, open people she'd met, all of them welcoming her as if she belonged. She bit her lip. "Unfortunately, I'll be gone by then."

"She leaves for L.A. next Monday," Fran explained. "Unless…"

Cinnamon didn't miss the sly glances Fran and the council members exchanged. "Unless what?" she asked.

Instead of answering, Anne smoothed the jacket of her navy wool suit and asked her own question. "Have you enjoyed your visit here?"

"Very much. Cranberry is beautiful, and the people are friendly." Especially Nick, who put a whole new spin on *friendly.*

"Pleased to hear that." Pete beamed as if she'd complimented his family. "We'd like to increase tourism, so spread that around, will you?"

"Here comes Mayor Jannings." Anne nodded at the portly, balding man striding toward them, his progress slowed by the people who greeted him. "He'll want to meet you."

Cinnamon barely had time to wonder why before the introductions took place.

"Any friend of Fran's is a friend of mine," the

mayor said. "I'm only sorry my wife isn't here. She'll be along shortly, though, and I know she'll be delighted to meet you."

It was almost as if they were wooing her. What for? Cinnamon eyed Fran suspiciously and earned an innocent smile.

"Well," Chet said, "we'd best head to the stage. Nice meeting you, Cinnamon, and again, welcome to Cranberry."

Pete, Anne and the mayor added similar comments. They drifted off, slowly making their way up the wooden steps to the podium and seats onstage.

A tingle climbed Cinnamon's spine and she sensed someone staring at her. Even before she glanced over her shoulder, she knew who it was.

Nick.

His forest-green flannel shirt flattered his dark complexion and brown eyes, but as his gaze locked on hers, her observations clouded. Catching her breath, she moved toward him.

NICK GAVE A MENTAL GROAN. He hadn't expected to see Cinnamon tonight—except in his imagination. Day and night she plagued his thoughts, keeping him miserably horny. No matter how often he told his brain he didn't want her, his body didn't give a penny nail's damn.

"Look—Fran and Cinnamon! Hi!" Abby raced toward them, deftly dodging people in her way.

Sharon followed, but Nick hung back, fighting a losing battle to keep his distance as Cinnamon's welcoming gaze pulled him toward her like an invisible string. Only when Abby prodded Cinnamon for attention did she switch her focus to his niece.

Trudging forward, hands curled into fists at his sides, he did the same. Anything to distract his mind and help him keep his hands off the woman whose kisses still burned in him.

Abby's little face beamed. "I really like the bookstore gift certificate. Mom's taking me there on Saturday. Thank you both so much."

"Yes, thank you," Sharon gushed, still aglow over her child's success despite the grave circumstances of the evening's town meeting. "Abby loves to read, and so do I."

"That's great," Cinnamon said. "Books have always been a huge part of my life. I couldn't live without them."

Nick didn't read unless forced. More the reason to keep his distance from her. As Cinnamon, Abby, Fran and Sharon discussed favorite books and authors, he hovered behind his sister, shifting uncomfortably and hoping nobody asked him for his favorites.

"Not only do you read a lot, but you're top in the state in math!" Fran grinned. "I feel as if I know a real celebrity."

Abby covered her mouth with her hand and giggled.

"Hey, can we sit with you?" Sharon asked, gesturing toward the empty seats in the front row.

Nick understood why those spaces were vacant. Most people hated to sit in the front, himself included. He would have preferred to lurk unnoticed in a corner in the back, with the crowd blocking Cinnamon from view. But with his sister and niece heading for the empty seats, he had no choice but to follow.

Sharon and Fran flanked Abby, leaving two chairs for Nick and Cinnamon.

"You and Cinnamon get to sit together," Abby said with a wide grin.

Cinnamon shot him a stricken look. He knew exactly how she felt. They were stuck side by side, which was pure torture. Wasn't tonight bad enough without this? He rolled his eyes.

Careful not to touch her—that would be dangerous—he sat down and offered her a stiff nod. "I didn't expect to see you here."

"Fran invited me," she replied, her gaze darting to her lap. Moments later she raised her head and looked at him. "About yesterday…"

She bit her sweet lower lip. He knew its softness and the taste of her mouth. Desire burned in his blood, and he barely stifled a groan. "What about yesterday?"

"I—"

Whatever she was about to day was cut off by the

loud squeak of a microphone. Standing at the podium, Mayor Jannings pushed a button, blew into the thing and tested it again. When all was well, he nodded at the crowd and offered a polite smile.

"Good evening and thank you for coming. What a great turnout, but that's one reason why I love this town. I know you love it, too. That's why the council members and I called this special meeting. We are in crisis, people. The Tate Cranberry Factory is on the brink of closing. It's my hope that together we'll figure out what we can do to save it, and tonight, I encourage you to share your ideas."

Nick noted Sharon's frown and Abby's grave expression. From his seat he couldn't reach either of them, yet he wanted to offer his sister a reassuring pat. Leaning back, he stretched his arm behind Cinnamon and touched Sharon's shoulder. She offered a wan smile.

He caught a whiff of Cinnamon's floral scent and inhaled, which caused his arm to brush her back. He pulled away, but the damage was done. His body went on red alert and the semierection that had plagued him all day threatened to go full tilt. She gave him a wide-eyed, accusing look that shamed him.

This was no time to think about sex. His sister's job was at stake. He angled away from her, desperate to shield his arousal and rein in his hunger.

He stared hard at the podium and strained to concentrate on Mayor Jannings. But nothing worked.

He was in lust hell, with no way out.

CINNAMON TRIED TO LISTEN to Mayor Jannings, but with Nick beside her, awareness of anyone else was difficult. Especially after he'd slipped his arm around her. She knew it was only to reach his sister, but the brief contact had aroused every nerve in her body. Now she longed to lean into him and exchange bone-melting kisses—and more.

Dear God. She locked her hands around her purse strap and shifted restlessly, her wooden folding chair creaking.

A grizzled man she recognized from the factory stood, and the mayor nodded at him. "Charlie?"

Determined to focus on the meeting instead of Nick, she swiveled her head toward the speaker.

"If we started earning a profit again, we'd do all right, wouldn't we?" he said.

"How're we going to do that, when our machinery is so durn old it breaks down constantly?" a man called out from the back. "We can't compete like this."

"You said it, Vince!" a woman shouted.

Angry people throughout the room yelled out thunderous agreement.

The mayor held up his hands for silence. "We can't discuss the problem if everybody talks at once," he stated loudly into the microphone. "One at a time, please. You'll all get your chance."

Hands shot into the air.

"Claude Jenkins has the floor."

The thin, graying man who stood appeared to be close to retirement age. "I've been with this factory forty-odd years and I've seen things go from good to okay to bad. I agree with Charlie, but I also agree with Vince. Given our situation, how're we going to make a profit?"

The man named Vince jumped to his feet. He was about Nick's age, with a stocky frame, wearing a Cranberry, Oregon, sweatshirt. "Even if Tate won't give us new machines, he oughta sink more money into advertising. That'd help."

"He hasn't bothered to do that over the past eight years. Why should he start now?" asked a middle-aged female with frizzy hair. "He's got a string of successful businesses. He doesn't need us. Unless we make money without his help, we're history."

"Ain't that the truth!" a woman shouted.

Grumbles again filled the room.

Vince, who was still standing, crossed his arms. "We don't even have a general manager anymore, just Andy, Claude and me trying to run the place without knowing what we're doing. Today the mixer jammed a good ten times. It's so old, nobody remembers how to do much except unclog it and pray. We had to close down one whole processing unit. Only the good Lord knows when we'll be able to use it again."

"Uncle Nick can fix that machine so it won't ever break again." Abby's girlish voice rang out. "Maybe he'll invent a whole machine like he did with the sorter my mom uses."

Nick, an inventor? Did he own the patent, and why hadn't he mentioned this talent? Cinnamon looked at him curiously.

"That's a great idea!" Sharon grinned at her brother.

Shouts of "Nick! Nick! Nick!" pounded through the room.

To Cinnamon's surprise his face flushed red and he ducked his head, as if he couldn't handle the attention. She'd never thought of him as shy. He certainly wasn't around Fran or her, and he hadn't been at Rosy's the other night. This was different.

"Stand up," Sharon urged.

"I think they want you to say something," Cinnamon added.

"No way, so both of you lay off."

He threw his sister a look Cinnamon couldn't see, then aimed a forbidding frown at her before his attention centered on his lap. Over his bent head Sharon raised her brow and shrugged.

Liz's brother stood. "Andy Jessup, here. You don't have to stand up or say anything, Nick. Just stop over to the factory tomorrow and give us a hand. We'll pay you out of the supplies fund, but don't tell Tate."

Nervous laughter erupted through the room, providing a needed respite from the tension and worry.

Nick eyed Fran, who expected him to return to work at the B and B in the morning. "My chores can wait," she said. "You go ahead and do what you can to help the factory."

He nodded. "I'll be over first thing tomorrow," he said loud enough for everyone to hear.

"Thanks," Andy called out.

A young woman with cocoa-colored skin stood. "I'm Becky Johnson and I run the sorter with Sharon Mahoney. Even if Nick fixes the problem, we'll be lucky to make up what we lost today, never mind turning a profit. You must know something we don't, Mayor Jannings. Are they gonna shut us down, and if so, when?"

"That's a fair question, Becky," the mayor said. "I spoke with Randall Tate this afternoon and asked him that very question. I also suggested he hire a consultant to help turn the business around. I recommended someone who happens to be sitting in the front row in this very room." He looked straight at Cinnamon. "Miss Cinnamon Smith, a close friend of Fran Bishop's, happens to be an expert at saving companies on the verge of bankruptcy. She's good at it, too. I checked."

Stunned, Cinnamon gaped at the man on stage while wild applause broke out.

"Wahoo," crowed Fran, shooting her a big grin.

Abby shrieked, and Sharon clapped louder than anyone else.

She frowned at Nick, who shrugged. "I had nothing to do with this, I swear," he said over the noise.

"I haven't finished," the mayor said in a booming voice. He looked and sounded so solemn, the crowd immediately quieted. "Unfortunately, due to cost considerations, Tate declined to hire Ms. Smith or any other consultant. He repeated what most of us already know—if he can't sell the factory over the next few months, he will shut it down."

Heavy silence greeted the statement, the tension and worry of the citizens of Cranberry palpable. Cinnamon felt awful for the people she'd come to know and like, especially Sharon, Abby and Nick. What would they do?

"Any nibbles from potential buyers?" a man asked from the back.

The grim-faced mayor shook his head. "Not as of this afternoon."

Nobody spoke, and the tension mounted. A tall woman in rimless glasses stood. "We're in a catch-22. Nobody wants to buy us because we're not profitable, but we won't be profitable until somebody sinks some money into the business."

"I have an idea," Cinnamon said in a voice only Fran, Sharon and Nick could hear. "What if—"

"Stand up and tell everyone," Fran urged.

Sharon nodded and glanced at Nick, who seconded the suggestion with a thumbs-up.

Cinnamon raised her hand.

"Our expert consultant has something to say," the mayor said.

She stood and pivoted to face the group. "Why don't the employees buy the factory?"

Stunned expressions greeted the question. "Interesting idea," the mayor said. "How would we go about doing that?"

"And how can we afford it, when most of us are struggling to make ends meet?" asked a woman a few rows back.

"You may not need much cash. There are attorneys who specialize in employee buyouts who could figure all that out." She glanced at Pete and Anne, seated on-stage. "Do either of you know of someone?"

The attorneys conferred quietly. "We might," Pete said. "First thing tomorrow, I'll check and report back to you."

"That'd be fine," Mayor Jannings said.

"Tate brought in his own general manager, but he quit," Andy said. "Our last local G.M. was Willis Tilden, and he's in the cemetery. There's nobody else around here to run the place."

The town council members exchanged blank looks, while from the floor, individuals fired off questions.

"How would our buying the place guarantee a profit?"

"What do we know about running a business?"

"How're we going to get money to upgrade our equipment?"

"What if we lose our shirts?"

From the back of the room, a rail-thin male who looked about sixteen stood. "My name's Eddie Wilkins," he said in a surprisingly powerful voice that boomed through the room. "I like your idea, Miss Smith. If you're Fran's friend, then I also trust you. Will you help us?"

Cinnamon considered the offer, which was exactly the kind of project she enjoyed. Earlier tonight, hadn't she wished she could stay here longer? Here was the chance to do that. Trouble was, she needed a job that paid decently. Working with factory employees who didn't have much to spare for a business teetering on bankruptcy, she'd be lucky to earn anything. How would she pay her bills and rebuild her savings? No, she couldn't accept. She opened her mouth to explain, but Fran cut her off.

"Cinnamon's services don't come cheap. She commands high fees and deserves every penny. How would we pay her?"

Cinnamon could have hugged her for stating her concerns.

"She needs to earn her living, just as we do," another understanding soul somewhere in the back called out.

The energy level in the room plummeted. Shoulders slumped and people stared desolately at their feet.

"You can have all the money in my savings account," Abby said as she scrambled to her feet. "Ninety-six dollars and fifty-three cents."

Heartfelt murmurs filled the room. Touched, Cinnamon smiled at the girl, whom she now liked and admired more than ever. "That's very sweet, Abby, but—"

"If the factory closes," the girl interrupted, the words tumbling over each other as if she were afraid slower speech might be easily stopped, "my mom and lots of her friends will lose their jobs. We'd have to move away, to a place where we don't know anybody." Chewing her thumbnail, she shot Cinnamon a stricken look. "I don't want to leave Cranberry and my friends, and I don't want to be the math bee champion for some other school. Most especially, I don't want to move away from my uncle Nick. He already told my mom and me he's not moving." Eyes huge and guileless, she finished. "Won't you please help us?"

The entire room went dead silent, everyone awaiting Cinnamon's answer. The plea deeply touched her. Her heart broke for the girl, her family and the friendly town. But much as she wanted to help, she couldn't survive without a decent pay-check.

She bit her lip. "I can't take your money, Abby."

Beside her, Nick cleared his throat. "Take mine, then. That machine I'm about to fix? Give my pay to Cinnamon."

Her jaw dropped as she turned toward him. His gaze held hers, warm and pleading. Before she could thank him and refuse, other offers peppered her.

"From now on you'll stay free at the Oceanside," Fran said.

"Eat anytime at Rosy's, on the house," the diner owner called out.

"That shin I patched up?" Doc said. "No charge."

"I'll give you free knitting lessons and all the complimentary yarn you need," Betsy promised.

"And free goodies from Cranberries-to-Go," Liz said.

Offers of free groceries, movie rentals and gas followed.

Cinnamon was awed by the generosity of these people, who didn't have much to begin with. Her knee-jerk response was to turn them down. Throughout her childhood she and her mother had lived hand-to-mouth, often relying on handouts. This wasn't charity, yet somehow it felt that way. Money was what she wanted and needed.

"Well?" Nick's soft words were for her ears only.

He didn't touch her, but he was so close she felt the warmth from his body. She wanted to look at him but didn't dare. She couldn't bear to see the disappointment on his face when she refused the job and let down the people of Cranberry.

She opened her mouth to refuse the offer. "All right, I'll help you," she said.

Shocked silent by her own words, she sat down hard, while cheers erupted and energetic conversation shook the rafters.

"Working without pay is not an option. I can't take this job," she stated, though over the noise she barely heard herself speak.

Apparently Nick heard, for his smile was warm and grateful. "I think you just did." Lifting her hand, he kissed her knuckles. "Thank you."

The warmth of his lips almost made up for the fear in her heart.

Chapter Ten

Thanks to noisy machinery, employees calling out to each other as they worked and oldies tunes belting from somebody's radio, Nick couldn't hear himself think. Lucky for him, installing the new rotator didn't call for much thought. That part of the job had come with studying the defective mixer and taking apart the engine yesterday, then spending all day and half the night designing and fashioning what he needed out of the odds and ends stashed in his workshop. Two whole days of work. He only hoped the thing ran.

If it did he'd get back to Fran's job and the other ones that paid, and get on with saving for Abby's camp room and board. Cinnamon said she didn't want his pay from this job, but he planned to give it to her anyway. He didn't begrudge her the money, since his first priority was doing what he could to help the factory survive.

Besides, the camp people had their deposit. They didn't want the rest until mid-July, a good five months from now. Plenty of time to save up—as long as Sharon didn't lose her job.

Nick slipped his screwdriver into his tool belt. He swiped his hands on his jeans, then he nodded to Cliff Baxter, the mix operator who, with his long neck and bobbing head, reminded Nick of a chicken.

Peering nervously at the control panel, Cliff waited until Nick joined him before pushing the start button. The engine purred to life, its huge metal blade rotating exactly as it should.

"She's good as new," Cliff hollered to his coworkers. "Thanks, buddy," he told Nick, clapping his shoulder.

"Happy to help," Nick replied.

His job here was finished. Employees around the area cheered and waved. Hating the attention, he accepted their thanks with a bowed head. Eager to head out, he pivoted toward the door on the other side of the factory.

He didn't move, though, because Cinnamon was walking toward him with the confident, sophisticated grace you'd expect of a woman with her smarts and background.

Dressed in expensive slacks and a matching sweater that hinted at her curves, she looked elegant and every inch the professional consultant, and out of place among the jeans-clad group.

While he was an unskilled, uneducated handyman in faded jeans and an old work shirt.

Aside from occasional glimpses of her moving through the factory interviewing workers and taking notes, he hadn't seen her since the town hall meeting two nights ago. But he'd thought about her nearly every waking moment, and plenty of sleeping ones, too. Now he drank in the sight of her, along with several other men on the floor. He scowled at the room in general, warning them off.

"Hello, Nick," she said, offering a cool, fleeting smile.

So she wasn't thrilled about running into him. He told himself he didn't care and hadn't expected anything else, especially since she was here more or less under forceful persuasion. Word was, she'd agreed to stick around two more weeks, then leave for good. Back to life in the big city.

Matching her reserved greeting, he offered a terse nod. "How's it going?"

"I could use a few more hours' sleep at night, but other than that, not bad."

He could identify with that. "I haven't been sleeping much, either," he admitted, glancing from her mouth to her eyes.

Cinnamon flushed, and for an instant her eyes darkened as they had after those kisses he couldn't seem to forget. With that one brief, hot look, the lust that had plagued him since she'd shown up at Fran's ignited. No way was he sprouting a hard-on here in the factory. Frowning, Nick backed up a few steps and reined in his desire.

"Sorry you took this job?" he asked.

She shook her head, surprising him. "Actually, I'm enjoying myself."

She noted the look on his face, and her lips twinged into a semblance of a smile. "That shocked me, too. I've been working late, researching the cranberry industry. I've learned interesting facts. Did you know that over the past decade, the world-wide demand for cranberry juice and frozen cranberries has dropped?"

"No, I didn't. We sure drink enough of the stuff around here."

"Apparently this town is the exception to the rule. In order to survive we need to look at manufacturing other cranberry products," she said. "Your sister and some of the other employees are meeting right now to brainstorm ideas."

Nick was impressed. "I don't think anybody ever asked them to do that."

"If they had, Tate's wouldn't be in the mess it is now. Employees are the experts. They'll come up with far better ideas than I ever could."

Nick never had considered that, but he certainly approved. He nodded. "What happens then?"

"We'll research the best product ideas. Then we'll add in the financial considerations and do some projections to make sure we're on the right track." She shrugged. "Then move forward."

Talking about these plans, she oozed enthusiasm. He couldn't stop a smile.

"What are you grinning about?" she asked, wrinkling her forehead.

"You look happy."

"I do love this kind of work."

"Ever consider going into business for yourself?"

Her eyes widened and he knew the question had caught her by surprise.

"Unlike you, I prefer a steady paycheck," she said. "Self-employment can't guarantee that."

"If you're trying to distract me with a dig, consider it heard and ignored. What are you scared of? With your attitude and brain it's a safe bet you'll have more work than you can handle."

"That's a risk I choose not to take," she said, the defensive lift of her head warning him to leave the matter alone.

He'd hit a nerve, though, and he stored away the information for later.

Silence hovered between them, broken by the whir and clang of machinery. Ready to leave, Nick jerked his head toward the exit. "I'll be going—"

"I found an attorney—"

They both spoke at the same time.

"What did you say?" Cinnamon asked.

"You first."

"I found a lawyer to help with the employee buy-out. He's coming here on Monday. Vince and Andy offered to sit in and represent everyone."

Nick nodded. "Sounds as if things are moving along."

"I'm pleased. You should be, too, for doing your part."

"You mean fixing the mixer? Piece of cake." He made a flip gesture with his hand. "Anybody could do it."

"That's not true. You have a gift, Nick, and you shouldn't dismiss it. I know people who'd kill to have your talent."

Acutely embarrassed and at the same time pleased at what she thought of him, he shoved his hands into his pockets. "Whatever."

Her eyes flashed and she opened her mouth. Nick knew what that meant. She was about to nag him about building his business.

He narrowed his eyes. "We through here?"

"A second ago you were going to say something."

"Not anymore."

"Well, then, do you have a minute? I'd like to discuss something with you. In private."

Damned if that last part didn't stir both his curiosity and his blood. "Private, huh?" He studied her from top to toe, enjoying the way she sucked in her stomach and pulled up her shoulders. "I like the sound of that."

The moment the words were out, he wanted to take them back. *Damn, Mahoney, get a grip.* No point flirting with a woman he'd never have.

Her cheeks flushed, and she looked more flustered than angry. Suddenly all business, she sighed. "I'm serious, Nick."

Following her lead, he sobered. "Talk away."

"Not here." She gestured him forward. "They're letting me use what was the general manager's office."

"What's this about?" he asked warily, quickening his stride to keep up with her.

"Come on and I'll tell you."

He followed her into the office.

OUTWARDLY CALM BUT INWARDLY shaking, Cinnamon preceded Nick into the cinder block office, wondering at her resolve. The man was more than skilled at designing and building machines. Yet he brushed off all praise. Out of modesty, or a total lack of interest? A week ago she'd have guessed lack of interest. But after observing his uptight reaction to attention and praise at the town meeting and also a few minutes ago, she wasn't certain.

He deserved recognition, money and more, and she was determined that he get it. Though what she was about to suggest could send him running, or make him as angry as when she'd mentioned building his business. Or maybe, being a laid-back male with no ambition, he simply wouldn't care.

Determined to keep things cordial and business-like, at least for now, she pasted a polite smile on her face and gestured at the coffeemaker on the waist-high counter lining one wall. "Would you like coffee?"

"No, thanks." Mouth quirking, Nick sank onto the lone visitor's chair across the desk, a sagging plaid-covered armchair that looked as uncomfortable as her wobbly, wooden desk chair. "I've tasted the stuff they call coffee around here. It's nasty."

As Cinnamon took her seat behind the scarred metal desk, she couldn't help laughing at his expression of disgust. "There's something we completely agree on."

They exchanged friendly grins that quickly sparked into more. Awareness sobered Nick's expression and smoldered in his eyes, and Cinnamon's nerves shifted into a different kind of tension.

Arm hooked casually over the back of his chair, he boldly studied her lips. Her mouth tingled. His avid gaze dipped to her breasts, which suddenly ached. When he lifted his attention to her face, his eyes burned with naked desire impossible to resist.

One word from him and she'd slip around the desk, sit on his lap and kiss him until they both were hot and breathless and ready for more…. Powerless to stop the responding hunger burning through her blood and hardly aware of her actions, Cinnamon heaved a sigh of longing and invitation.

Nick swore, jerked his posture upright and glanced at the stained teal carpet. "What's this about?" he asked in a gruff voice.

Dear God, she'd practically propositioned him! Self-conscious and embarrassed, she straightened the papers on her desk. *He's not what I want,* she silently reminded herself. Besides, she was too busy for anything but her work with the factory. What happened in this office was business, period.

"The sorter you designed is impressive," she said. "Simple yet ingenious. Wherever did you get the idea?"

His modest shrug was just what she expected. "The one Sharon operated kept breaking down, so I invented something better. To make her job easier."

"You certainly did." About to tread on delicate matters, Cinnamon posed a question she already knew the answer to. "I assume you were paid well for your work?"

He shook his head. "I didn't do it for the money, I did it to help Sharon. Tate never even knew."

"That's not fair to you." Fingers laced together atop the desk, she leaned forward. "Have you at least applied for a patent?"

The question earned her an are-you-crazy look. "No. Why?"

"You designed a piece of equipment that, from what my research shows, is more efficient than any other sorter in use. You ought to get paid for that."

"Right. The factory can't even pay *you*. How would it pay me?"

"Since the factory makes some of its money thanks to you, it should compensate you. Once the employees take over and the company begins to turn a profit, you deserve a percentage of that. This same scenario ought to apply to any factory in the country, or the world, for that matter, that uses the machine you invented. You can earn royalties, Nick, potentially a good deal of money."

His turn to lean forward, his face reflecting confusion and disbelief. "I don't see how."

"The way it works is, if you hold the patent and this or any other business chooses to use your design, they pay you for the privilege. Otherwise they're taking your genius and profiting from it, while you get nothing."

"I'm no genius," he said, flushing, "but I do want that money. How do I collect?"

The question meant he'd accept her suggestion and run with it instead of getting upset. Cinnamon jumped eagerly into consultant mode. "For starters, you file for a patent." She handed him the papers she'd prepared earlier. "I downloaded the forms and printed off two copies of everything. All you have to do is read through the documents and fill them out."

At his stricken look, she hurried on. "This is something you can do on your own, but if I were you, I'd get legal counsel before sending anything to the U.S. Patent Office. Now, I contacted Pete and Anne, and they suggested an attorney who—"

"You what?" Nick's eyes narrowed ominously.

Uh-oh. Cinnamon swallowed, but it was to late to stop now. Besides, she saw nothing wrong with what she'd said or done, and refused to be intimidated.

She forced a calming breath. "I asked Pete and Anne for the name of a good patent attorney around here. The closest person they know lives about sixty miles away. That's a long drive, I know, but at least you don't have to go all the way to Portland." She slid a slip of paper across the desk. "Here's her number."

Nick ignored it. Expression dark and forbidding, he crossed his hands over his chest. "Did I ask you to do that?"

"No, but I thought—"

"You didn't think at all." The small tic she was starting to know so well pulsed in his jaw. "If I wanted your help I'd ask for it." He pushed to his feet. "I don't."

With a curt nod he snatched up the papers and phone number, then pivoted toward the exit. He strode from her office, slamming the door behind him.

"THEN HE STORMED OUT," Cinnamon told Fran that evening over chicken and dumplings. Tonight they were eating in the dining room at home. "I seem to have a knack for making him mad."

Recalling the harsh set of his shoulders and flash-ing eyes, Cinnamon winced. At least he'd taken the papers. Mission accomplished, right? And she felt awful.

Appetite ruined, she pushed aside her plate. "What should I do, Fran? I don't want him angry at me."

"Nick's a very private person. Maybe he doesn't like you nosing into his personal affairs. If the situa-tions were reversed and he was poking into your life, how would you feel?"

A few days back, he'd posed a similar question. She should have listened more carefully, Cinnamon realized. "When you put it that way…" She gave a sheepish shrug. "Really, I was only trying to help. Nick deserves money and recognition for his inven-tion. He won't go after those things without a push."

"All true," Fran mused. A beat later she canted her head and narrowed her eyes at Cinnamon. "But are you sure about your motives?"

Cinnamon frowned. "What are you getting at?"

"You're starting to care about him."

"Only as a friend," Cinnamon quickly assured Fran. She even looked her in the eye.

Yet deep down, she knew different. She really *was* starting to care for Nick as more than a friend. That scared her even more than not having a job lined up.

ALONE IN HIS SMALL KITCHEN, Nick hunched over the patent registration papers he'd been working through the whole evening. Yawning, he massaged his aching neck and glanced at the round clock that hung on the wall. Close to midnight. No wonder his neck had a crick in it.

He frowned at the papers spread out on the table. Four hours spent deciphering what looked like hieroglyphics and he'd plowed through a whopping two pages of instructions, reading and rereading until it made sense. He'd managed to fill out most of one page. Only a few million to go.

You're not stupid, you just see words differently than most people. That's what Mr. Edison had said back in high school. Maybe that was true, but at the moment Nick felt pretty damn thickheaded. And fed up.

At this rate he might finish by Christmas. If he was lucky. Unfortunately, that was ten months away and he didn't have that kind of time.

Sharon could help. As soon as the thought entered his head he shut it down. His sister barely had time for her own bills and paperwork without taking on his, too. Then there was nosy little Abby, who might wonder why he wasn't doing the work himself, or worse, tell somebody her uncle couldn't take care of his own business.

Nick squirmed at the thought. He'd rather swallow battery acid than have his niece or anyone else know he found reading so hard. Especially Cinnamon.

In his mind he saw her face, warm and admiring as

she praised his sorter invention and the mixer repair. That had felt good, and remembering the conversation now wasn't bad, either. He smiled, until he considered what she'd do if she found out he couldn't read. For sure she'd never look at him like that again. Likely she'd never look at him at all.

Damn her for poking her nose where she had no business sticking it and shackling him with work he had no time for. In a fit of frustration he swore, crumpled the nearly completed page into a ball and lobbed it into the trash can.

Instantly he regretted the action.

What about the money? Cinnamon said he stood to earn a bunch. If she said so, he believed her.

He sure as hell needed money, for Abby's camp and her college tuition. He wouldn't mind paying off Sharon's debts, too, and making her life easier.

Not gonna happen without that patent.

His gaze homed in on the paper with the patent lawyer's phone number. He'd ask the expert for help. Cinnamon had said *she* would, right?

But asking a lawyer to do what he should take care of himself would cost plenty. He'd save money and bring her the completed paperwork. Then get her advice.

Nothing to do but buckle down and finish the sucker. He retrieved the crumpled paper and smoothed it out. Rubbing his tired eyes, he bent again to his work.

Chapter Eleven

Late Monday afternoon, fresh from a trip to the patent lawyer's and ridiculously pleased with himself, Nick strode toward Cinnamon's office. The door was closed. He was in such good spirits he didn't let that stop him. He knocked, then opened it.

She was squinting at her laptop sitting on the battered, old desk that should have been tossed on the scrap heap.

"Hey," he said, pausing in the threshold. "You busy?"

Her eyes widened and she looked a little scared. "That depends on why you're here. Are you going to bawl me out again?"

Nothing could dampen his high spirits. "Why, have you poked your nose into more of my business?" he asked, tempering the words with a half smile.

"I think I learned my lesson on that." She closed the laptop. "I'm sorry, Nick. I shouldn't have pushed you."

"As long as you learned your lesson," he teased, no longer upset. "Now can I come in?"

She nodded, and he strode inside, closing the door behind him. Whistling softly, he sauntered over.

"Please, sit down," Cinnamon said, indicating the chair across the desk.

Not wanting to take up her time, he shook his head. "I'm only here for a few minutes. I just got back from the patent lawyer," he proudly announced.

"You did?"

Considering the way he'd stormed out of her office last Thursday, her obvious surprise made sense. "Based on your advice," he said, feigning innocence. "The lawyer checked the application and said everything looked fine. She'll do a search to make sure no one else holds a patent on my invention. Then she'll mail it in."

Cinnamon beamed. "That's wonderful news."

"Yeah, it is." He grinned back like a fool. "I told her about some of my other inventions and she said she'd research them, too."

"There are others?"

Her astonishment tickled him. "Six more," he said, puffing out his chest. "Anyway, that's what I came to tell you. I'll let you get back to your work."

"Wait." She rose and came around the desk. "You're an amazing and talented man, Nick Mahoney."

The high praise felt damned good. "Thanks," he said.

He let his gaze comb over her. As usual, she looked beautiful. His body stirred to life the way it always did around her.

He knew he should fight his need, but he was flush with his success. "You're not so bad yourself," he drawled.

On cue her cheeks pinkened as she extended her hand. "Congratulations."

Instead of shaking it, he threaded his fingers through hers. "I'm not some casual business associate," he said, caressing her thumb with his.

Her eyes darkened, and he saw that this small touch aroused her as much as it did him. He tugged her hand, bringing her closer.

She raised her head and her lips parted, an invitation tough to resist. But moving forward could be dangerous. There was too much heat between them, and once they started, there was no guarantee he could stop—and no way to keep his heart from getting trampled when she discovered he was a fraud. And sooner or later she would.

"Nick?" She searched his face. "What's happening between us?"

He'd never noticed the tiny silver flecks in her eyes. As he delved into those rust-colored depths, they seemed to shimmer and beckon him closer. Lust swirled in his head, fogging his common sense. He swallowed. "I don't know." With his free hand he cupped her chin, ensuring that her eyes met his. "But I can't stop thinking about kissing you again."

A shallow, rapid breath whispered from her lips, and under his palm her pulse jumped. A certain part of him stirred to life.

"Is that so?" she asked.

He drank in her open, yearning expression. "Admit it, you want the same thing I do."

"This pull between us is dangerous. You should go," her mouth said, but her flushed skin and hungry eyes told him something different.

Her flowery scent stirred his senses. He had to taste her. "Just one 'congratulations' kiss," he urged, his thumb caressing the soft skin of her cheek. "Then I swear I'll leave."

Her head tilted back a fraction and her pupils grew big, silent but potent signs that she wanted what he did.

"One kiss, then," she agreed in a breathy, husky voice.

Her eyelids dropped, shielding her eyes, and her palms slid to his shoulders. She settled against his chest, her cheek over his heart, soft curves tantalizing the hard planes of his body.

A warm sound purled from his chest. "Damn, you feel good."

She sighed. "Same here."

Her hips pressed close, nuzzling and tempting. Heat throbbed in his groin and he knew she felt his arousal.

"You were right. This is dangerous," he growled, grasping her hips. "But right now I don't care."

"Neither do I." She framed his face between her warm, incredibly sensual hands. "Kiss me, Nick."

He dipped his head and did just that.

BLOOD ROARED IN NICK'S head as Cinnamon tangled her tongue with his. These kisses were even hotter than before, and he wanted to get her naked and sink into her sweetness. *Now.* Instead he forced himself to slow down.

Hard and throbbing with need, he gripped her soft, round behind and pulled her tight to his erection. She made throaty little sounds, as titillating as a touch.

"My legs are about to buckle," she sighed against his lips.

Tearing his mouth from hers, chest heaving, he glanced around the room. Wobbly chairs, metal desk, stained carpet. He refused to stoop that low. "Let's try the counter—"

"How about the counter—" she suggested at the same time.

They both laughed, and he grabbed her hand and pulled her toward the far wall.

Cinnamon pushed the coffeemaker aside. Nick lifted her up. "Now, where were we?" he asked.

She wrapped her thighs around his hips so that the sweetest part of her fitted against his need. "Right *there*, I think."

Her boldness turned him on even more. In a haze of desire he kissed her—deep, demanding kisses she eagerly returned. He shifted closer—as close as two fully clothed people could get. It wasn't enough.

Desperate to touch her, he slid his hands under her sweater and up her smooth, slender back. His trembling hands moved to her breasts.

Catching her breath, she edged back, allowing him room to cup and hold her. Her nipples were swollen and stiff. He squeezed gently, gratified when she moaned with pleasure.

"You are so sweet," he murmured. "And it's awfully hot in here. Why don't you get rid of that sweater?"

Eyes locked on his, she pulled the turtleneck over her head, revealing a sexy, pink lace bra that fastened in the front.

"Nice bra," he said, "but it has to go. I've been imagining what your breasts looked like since that day you fell and hurt your shin."

"That's a long time." Offering the smile of a woman fully aware of her sexual power, she unhooked the bra and removed it. He stared openly at her small but perfect breasts, the nipples sharp and a dusky pink.

"Are they what you imagined?" she asked, cupping herself.

Nick groaned. "Better by a long shot. I wonder if they taste as good as they look." Bending down, he licked each taut peak, teasing his tongue slowly over the sensitive tips.

The throaty noise started again. As he gently suckled and nipped, Cinnamon tensed and gripped his shoulders. Pleasure pounded through him, and he wanted her so much it scared him. And jerked him to his senses.

What in hell was he doing? This wasn't supposed to happen.

He straightened and backed away. "Uh, that's all the congratulations I can handle."

By the dazed expression on her face he wasn't sure she understood. Her hair was wildly messy, and her face, neck, breasts and lips were flushed—as if he'd made love with her.

And, heaven help him, he wanted to do just that.

"Better get dressed," he ordered in a gruff voice.

"Right." Gaze averted, she covered her breasts with her hands. "Please hand me my clothes."

He retrieved the bra and sweater from the floor. Afraid to touch her, he set them on the counter beside her.

"What we just did… I didn't mean for it to happen," he said, locking his hands behind his back.

"We're both at fault."

Knowing he should apologize but not sorry for anything that had happened, he started toward the exit.

"Don't you dare open that door until I'm dressed."

"Brother," he muttered, but she had a point. He glanced at his swollen groin and figured he ought to wait a moment, too. Facing the door, he couldn't see her. But he heard her every move and pictured her clearly in his mind.

Her feet hit the carpet with barely a sound. A moment later he heard the no-nonsense click of her bra, followed by the swish of her sweater as she pulled it over her head and smoothed it down.

"All right, I'm decent."

He turned toward her. With or without her top, she looked like a woman thoroughly loved. "If I were you I'd comb my hair and fix my makeup," he advised.

"Thanks. I will." All business now, as if that could erase what had just happened, she waved at the door. "Goodbye, Nick, and once again, congratulations on filing the patent."

Dipping his chin, he acknowledged her good wishes. "See you around."

He walked out, closing the door behind him.

STANDING AT THE SORTER, Becky Johnson, who worked with Sharon, nudged her. "Look who just came out of Cinnamon's office."

Sharon pushed the stop button, then jerked her attention across the floor. "What's Nick doing here? He didn't mention coming in today." Frowning at her brother's set jaw, she adjusted the hairnet her work required her to wear for sanitary reasons. "What do you think happened in there?"

"I don't know, but the man looks as if he just swallowed a pint of cranberry juice that turned to vinegar."

"I can't imagine why." Sharon puzzled. "He fixed the mixer and designed us a better sorter. Other than those things he has nothing to do with this place, and as far as I know, nothing to do with Cinnamon."

"Well, they must have had words about something." Hands on her ample hips, Becky shook her head, her face worried.

Nick's sister sighed. "You know, I dearly love my brother. I like Cinnamon, too, and I believe she's going to save this place. For the sake of the factory and our jobs, those two had better get along."

"Get *along?*" Becky laughed. "Are you blind, girl? Have you seen the way he checks her out when she isn't looking? Or that hungry look on her face whenever he walks into a room? Honey, they ought to get *together.*"

"I don't know," Sharon said. "Nick doesn't get close to anybody."

"Well, it's clear as a juice bottle he wants to get close to Cinnamon. Only, maybe he doesn't know it."

At the gleam in Becky's eyes, Sharon grinned. "Hmm… We could help them along."

"Now we're working on the same machine. Whatcha got in mind?"

"I don't know, but I think I'll pay Fran a visit."

WEDNESDAY MORNING, RAIN spattered the windows of Cinnamon's suite, and the wind howled. But the crackling fire that warmed the small living room made up for the bad weather.

A brisk knock sounded at the door. "It's Fran."

"Come in." Sitting at the desk facing the window, Cinnamon saved the work on her laptop and twisted toward the door.

When Fran entered, her purple overalls and tangerine turtleneck seemed to brighten up the gray day. "You look like spring."

"Wishful thinking. I'm about to leave for the town hall to finalize the decorations for Saturday's Valentine's Day dance. I'll be gone awhile."

Cinnamon gestured at her laptop. "I'm sure that when you get back I'll still be here, working." The factory projections weren't right, and she'd brought the spreadsheets home to rework them.

"There's a fresh pot of coffee downstairs if you want it."

"Thanks. Have fun."

Instead of leaving, her friend hesitated, a guilty look on her face.

"What?" Cinnamon asked.

"Did I mention that Nick will be here soon, to fix your ceiling fan?"

He was the last person Cinnamon wanted to see, and she couldn't stem an unhappy frown.

Fran didn't know that. She didn't know about those kisses and more, because Cinnamon hadn't told her. She must have suspected something had gone wrong, though, for every time she mentioned Nick's name, Cinnamon changed the subject. That explained the guilty expression.

"Why didn't you tell me he was coming? I could have worked at the factory today."

And to avoid him, she would have.

She couldn't believe what she and Nick had done. And in her office, too, where anybody could have walked in! But one kiss and she'd forgotten everything and would have gladly made love with the man...if he hadn't come to his senses and stopped. Thank God he had, for making love with him would have been a big mistake. They weren't right for each other, and she already cared more than she should. Making love would only deepen her feelings.

"Go out in this weather, when you don't have to? Bad enough one of us is forced to brave the elements." Fran shook her head. "For the past week you've spent ten hours a day at Tate's, including last weekend. You deserve to stay right here in front of the fire. Nick won't bite, you know."

Oh, but he did—light nips that set her body on fire. He sure could kiss, too. And taste and lick...

Her body burned with longing. Three days away from the man and she ached for him. Last night she'd even clutched her pillow, wanting him more than she'd ever wanted anyone.

Not wise, and she truly did not want to see him. She closed the laptop and stood. "I think I'll take a break."

Fran's expression was wary. "You're not going running again, are you? Your shin is barely healed, and even with the nonskid strips on the steps, you could slip."

She recalled Nick's seductive words: "I've been imagining what your breasts looked like since that day you fell and hurt your shin." And his expression—eyes dark and hot, mouth slightly open—before he laved her sensitive nipples... Cinnamon's most sensitive place warmed and dampened. Heaven help her.

Hugging herself, she shook her head. "Don't worry, I learned my lesson about running in a downpour. I think I'll browse the bookcase downstairs, find a good novel and lose myself in it. That way I'll be out of Nick's way when he shows up."

Given the way her common sense disappeared whenever the man was near—actually, whenever she thought about him—keeping out of his way seemed a smart plan, indeed.

The furtive look on her friend's face caused Cinnamon to eye her suspiciously. "What *now?*"

"It's just that you seem angry at him. This is a good opportunity for you two to talk, and straighten out whatever caused the problem."

"I'm not mad." Turning toward the sliding glass doors leading to her balcony, Cinnamon stared at the foaming waves. Now, *they* looked angry. A heavy sigh slipped from her lips before she again faced Fran. "But there is a problem," she admitted. "You were right. I'm starting to feel things for Nick I don't want to feel."

"I *knew* it!"

Cinnamon frowned. "Don't look so darned pleased, because I don't intend to act on my emotions." Not as long as she kept her distance.

"But Nick's a terrific guy. And now, with more than one invention soon to be patented, he'll soon meet your requirements for a man with money in the bank. Because I'm certain he'll earn plenty."

Cinnamon was, too. Maybe he wasn't the white-collar executive she pictured in her life, but he was an inventor, and creative people didn't work regular hours.

And why was she thinking like this? She was leaving town a week from tomorrow. Besides, Nick wasn't right for her and she wasn't right for him. Irritated with herself and her interfering friend, she rolled her eyes. "You missed your calling, Fran. You should be in the matchmaking business."

Fran widened her eyes innocently. "I'm only stating the facts. Don't forget about the Valentine's Day dance Saturday night. Nick will be there, and with love in the air that night, who knows what will happen?"

Cinnamon released an exasperated sigh. "You don't give up, do you? I'm not sure I'm going to that dance. I will be visiting the Love on Main Street outdoor art show, though. Maybe I'll even buy something."

Dipping deeper into her dwindling savings would hurt, but she couldn't imagine leaving Cranberry without some memento. At the moment she couldn't imagine leaving Cranberry, period. What the town lacked in ammenties it more than made up for in warmth. Cranberry and many of the people in it had taken root in her heart.

"You'll love the art show, and I'm glad you're going," Fran said. "But you can't miss the dance. It's a huge event. Everybody in town goes, including the tourists. Since I'm one of the organizers and chair of the decorations and entertainment committees, it'd mean a lot to me if you came." She looked sideways at Cinnamon. "Besides, we're making a big fuss over Abby that night. You can't miss that."

Cinnamon laughed. "All right, I'm sold. Just don't expect anything to happen between Nick and me."

"Okay," Fran said. "You know, you could stay longer. Unless that consulting firm in Boston hires you."

A few days earlier a company Cinnamon had queried via e-mail had contacted and interviewed her by phone. Happily, they seemed to care more about her skills and experience than her romantic relationship with her former boss. "I expect a job offer soon."

Given her attachment to Cranberry, that didn't feel as good as it should. But without job opportunities here, she couldn't think of staying.

"I thought so." Fran nodded. "I'm happy for you, but depressed for me. I'll miss you."

"I know," Cinnamon said. "But we have another full week, which is longer than I originally meant to stay."

"For which I and the town of Cranberry are more than grateful." Suddenly Fran cocked her head. "I think I heard Nick come in."

Too late to hide now, and besides, Cinnamon was no coward. She'd say hello and then head downstairs, find that book and hide…er, read in the great room. "Please don't tell him what I said."

"Never, hon. That's up to you." Fran moved to the door. "I'll see you late this afternoon." She winked. "Have fun with Nick."

"Fran!" Cinnamon felt her cheeks warm. "You're impossible."

She barely had time to straighten her papers and fluff her hair before he appeared in her doorway.

Dressed in jeans and a flannel shirt, tool belt on his hips, he carried a stepladder under his arm. Raindrops glistened in his windblown hair, and his face was ruddy from the rain, cold and wind. He easily could have posed as a model for an outdoorsmen's calendar. In a word, he was gorgeous.

Her body went into its now-familiar routine — nerves on edge, breasts sensitive, place between her legs pulsing. "Hello," she said, sounding breathless to her own ears.

"You're not supposed to be here." His eyes roved slowly over her face and body, as if he knew where she most wanted his touch.

"Yes," she murmured, hardly aware she'd spoken.

The word put a stop to his blatant stare. He blinked, and the warmth in his eyes was gone, as if she'd imagined it. "I'm here to fix the fan," he said without a trace of interest.

As if he'd never kissed her, never seen her bare breasts or touched or tasted them. As if he didn't want to, ever again.

Oh, that hurt. Then again, this was a whole lot safer. Still her traitorous body yearned toward him, her foolish fingers itching to clasp his neck and urge his face close enough to kiss.

Afraid she might do exactly that, she picked up her laptop and hugged it to her chest. "Don't let me stop you," she said, matching her cool tone to his.

Chapter Twelve

"You hugging that laptop because you love it, or to protect yourself?" Nick asked as he set the ladder beneath the fan.

She *was* holding it like a shield, Cinnamon realized. She returned it to the desk, then raised her chin. "I don't need protecting." She lied because she clearly did—from her own misguided longings for Nick Mahoney.

In an effort to stifle the hunger raging through her, she backed away from the man.

"Relax," he said, misinterpreting her action. "I'm not about to kiss you again." His neutral expression said he meant that.

"That's a relief." Another lie.

Disappointment settled heavily in her chest, but at least she knew the truth—she was out of Nick's system. Too bad he wasn't out of hers.

He unbuckled the tool belt, the casual act somehow

so intimate she blushed clear to her toes. "Wh-what are you doing?" she asked as he laid it on the carpet.

"Looking at that fan—" he pointed upward "—I see that I don't need my tools to take it down, just my hands."

He flexed his fingers, big and callused, but so very skilled at stroking and fondling....

Her breasts tightened, craving his touch. "I see." Fighting the urge to invite him to take up where he'd left off two days ago, she glanced around the room. "You did a nice job with the paint touch-ups. And the windows sparkle. Fran's Valentine's Day guests are sure to be impressed."

Months ago, a couple eager to spend the holiday weekend here had reserved the Orca suite. For that matter, every room in the Oceanside was booked.

Nick nodded. "This suite is always rented."

"That's understandable," Cinnamon said, glancing around. "This is a place for lovers."

The word hung in the air between them, a painful reminder of her sexual desire. If only she could call it back.

Nick swallowed hard, as if his throat were dry. With his mouth tight and his eyes narrowed, he chipped at a paint stain on the ladder. "With every room taken over the Valentine's Day weekend, where will you stay?"

"Starting tomorrow night I'll be sleeping in Fran's

spare bedroom. Monday, after the guests check out and the room is cleaned, I'll move back up here."

Leaving the paint stain alone, he nodded. Cinnamon couldn't read his expression, but the tension radiating from him was as real as the ladder.

She was equally uncomfortable, and she moved toward the door. "I'll go now and leave you in peace. If you need anything, I'll be downstairs reading."

"Peace, huh?" He laughed without humor. "That's a good one."

Before she could ask him what he meant, he turned his back and climbed the ladder.

She fled.

STANDING ON THE MIDDLE step of the ladder, Nick swore as he stretched up to unscrew the fan. Here he was, supposed to be working, and so damn horny he could hardly focus. His arousal strained uncomfortably against his Levi's, but lately that was his normal state, and he was getting used to it.

Good thing Fran couldn't see him now. Or Cinnamon.

He wanted her so badly it hurt. He was no expert on women, but she was easy to understand. Those soft sighs and longing glances left little doubt that she wanted him, too.

She's right downstairs. All I have to do is head down there, pull her close und...

"Like hell." Setting his jaw, he stifled his thoughts.

Unfortunately, his body remained taut and aroused. Damn, but it was hard to fight this.

Eight days and she'd be gone. Until then he'd try like hell to steer clear of her. Or if he had to be around her, pretend he didn't want her, just as he had a few minutes ago.

Piece of cake. He scowled at his bulging jeans. "Got that?"

CURLED UP IN A large armchair, Cinnamon stared at the pages of the best-seller mystery that promised to grab her attention. Unfortunately it wasn't working. She couldn't concentrate, not with Nick upstairs.

Had she really told Betsy and Liz she didn't want a fling with him? Because she did. With her body hungry and her mind full of the man, would it be so wrong to enjoy a short-term, no-strings affair? No, she decided, as long as she was careful to keep her heart out of the equation.

She could do that. Couldn't she?

No point even wondering, since Nick no longer seemed interested.

Restless and edgy, Cinnamon tossed aside the book and frowned. The man had been up there nearly an hour. How long could fixing a fan take?

Her "break" was over, and she wanted to get back to work. She'd go to the factory after all, where she could concentrate. But she needed her laptop and purse, and they were in the suite.

She marched upstairs with her stomach in knots. "Don't be silly," she murmured. "You're not going up there to seduce him, only to get your things."

When she arrived, the fan was making lazy circles in the room, stirring the fire-warmed air. Arm hung over the ladder, eyes on the ceiling, Nick nodded without glancing at her. "The fan works fine now. I'm through here."

"Great."

He'd be out of the room soon, then. She could stay here, if she wanted, but she was restless and needed a change of scenery. She headed into the bedroom and retrieved her purse from the bedside table. Slinging it over her shoulder, she strode to the desk, where she'd left the laptop. "I'm going to the factory."

That earned a curious look. "Dressed like that?"

Frowning, she set down her things to check the zipper of her jeans—closed—and smooth her dove-gray turtleneck sweater over her hips. "Is there something wrong with my clothes?" she asked, glancing up.

He was watching her through hooded eyes. He jerked as if she'd caught him stealing. He shook his head. "Not a thing, but you usually dress up when you work."

"You think I should change into nicer clothes before I go?"

"Change?" he said, voice cracking.

Eyes naked with hunger burned into her, and she knew that he still wanted her as badly as she wanted him. She couldn't look away, couldn't stop the soft moan that slipped from her lips.

"Sharon says," he started. Stopped and cleared his throat. "She says you, Vince and Andy met with a lawyer about the employee buyout."

"We did." She managed a casual nod at odds with her pounding heart. "A buyout definitely is doable. It's complicated. But the way I understand it, employees will buy into the company using part of each paycheck to purchase shares. The bank is involved, too, with financing. We meet with everyone tomorrow to answer questions and vote. Then our attorney will take the offer to Tate's attorney."

"That's good news. Thank you for what you've done."

"You're welcome."

If only he'd stop looking at her as if he wanted to make love to her.

The need inside her grew unbearable. Hardly aware of her actions, she moistened her lips with her tongue and strained toward him. "Yesterday I had a phone interview with a consulting company in Boston."

His hot, avid gaze dipped to her mouth. "And?"

"I don't know," she replied honestly. "I need that job, but I really like it here." *I really like you, Nick.*

In an instant she made up her mind. She wanted to make love with him, and would, right now. An affair never to be forgotten.

Before she could chicken out she pulled her sweater over her head and moved purposefully toward him.

A strangled sound burst from his throat. "This thing between us is killing me. I can't fight it alone, Cinnamon."

"Then don't fight at all."

She walked into his arms. Then he was kissing her urgently, as if she were water and he was dying of thirst. Her body throbbed and screamed for release, and she was sure she'd be the one to die if they didn't make love.

She lost herself in sensation and need. Somehow they were on the bed and her bra was gone.

Thanks to the fire and the thick down comforter beneath her, she was warm and cozy. Thanks to Nick, she was hot and needy.

Kneeling between her open legs Nick licked her breasts, first teasing and gentle, then, when she squirmed for more, nipping harder. Wild with need and desperate for more, she wrapped her thighs around his hips and pulled him hard against the pulsing nub that demanded attention.

"Easy," he cautioned, bracing his weight on his elbows.

"I want you, Nick," she said.

His eyes went hot. "And I want you naked."

Rolling to his side, he unfastened the button and zipper of her jeans. She lifted her hips and helped him strip off her jeans and bikini panties. At last she was naked. Pulsing and ready, she waited for him to join her.

Nick stared down at her, his face dark and intent, the desire plain. "You are so beautiful."

Eyes closed, he feathered his fingers from her collarbone, tantalizingly slowly across each nipple, and down her stomach.

She wished he'd take off his clothes, but the haze of her need clouded her brain. She'd die if he didn't touch her *there*. She raised her hips in supplication. "Please, Nick."

He laughed softly. "I'll get there."

At last his fingers slid below her navel. Cinnamon sucked in a breath, and finally, finally he slipped his hand between her legs. Quivering with need and anticipation, she moaned.

"You're slick and wet," he growled with satisfaction.

"For you." She pulled his head down and kissed him with all the passion she felt.

Parrying his tongue with hers, he slid two fingers inside her, his thumb teasing the heart of her desire. Pleasure pounded through her, exquisite to the point of pain.

"Ohh," she whimpered, writhing against his hand.

"Like that, huh?"

"No. Yes." Breathing hard she stilled. "It's been a while and I'm afraid… I mean… I'm close to—"

"Climaxing? Let it happen, honey."

"What about you?" she managed, his clever fingers making the words hard to say.

"Forget me, Cinnamon. This is for you."

There was no way she could fight her need. Her eyelids drifted closed. Low in her belly, tension and longing spiraled higher and tighter.

He knew exactly what she needed, stroking and increasing pressure until she cried out and came apart.

When she drifted back to earth she drew in a shuddering breath and smiled into Nick's eyes. "That was amazing."

"My pleasure," he murmured. "I enjoyed watching you."

She was too content to feel embarrassed.

But it wasn't fair that he was still dressed.

She sat up and gestured for him to do the same. His eyebrows arched, but he obeyed. Wordlessly she worked the buttons of his shirt, pausing to stroke his chest. Beneath her hand his heart thudded wildly. She pushed the soft flannel off his shoulders and tossed the shirt onto the carpet. She ran her hands over his broad shoulders and down his solid chest. He was perfect, hard and muscled and beautiful.

She wanted him inside her.

On her knees now, holding onto his shoulders she licked his nipples, mimicking what he'd done to her. He groaned, and she smiled to herself. She kissed his rib cage, then his navel. Nick went still.

As she reached for his zipper, he grasped her wrist and stopped her.

"Better not." Breathing hard, he rolled out of reach.

This was the second time he'd stopped.

"What's wrong?" Puzzled, and suddenly embarrassed at her nudity, Cinnamon wriggled under the covers. She pulled up the comforter, tucking it under her armpits. "Is it me?"

While Nick retrieved his shirt from the floor, she leaned against the hard wooden headboard. He shook his head, then shrugged into his shirt. "You're amazing."

"Then is it a religious thing, or do you have a disease?"

He almost smiled. "No to both. I just don't think we should make love."

"We're both single and unattached, so why not?"

"For starters, I don't have birth control with me."

Was that all? "That's okay. I'm on the pill."

She gave him a hopeful glance. But he dashed her hope with a frown and a muttered oath.

"What did you say?" she asked.

"This is more complicated than birth control." He propped himself against the headboard beside her.

"I've been tested for all the diseases. I'm clean."

"Me, too, but that's not what I'm talking about. You're an educated executive and I'm a handyman," he said as he buttoned his shirt. "We're not a good fit."

A similar argument to the one Cinnamon had told herself. But she no longer believed it. "A few minutes ago we seemed to fit fine," she said. "We share this strong attraction we can't seem to fight. And you're far more than a handyman," she corrected. "You're a gifted inventor with a talent for fixing just about anything."

"Think what you want." He waved off the compliments, the same as he always did. "There are things you don't know about me."

"I'm pretty open-minded," she coaxed, turning to touch his cheek. "Try me."

Pain and self-doubt filled his eyes before he pulled away from her. He crossed his arms, and his mouth tightened stubbornly. He wasn't going to confide in her.

Stifling a frustrated sigh, she tried again. "Keep your secrets, then. You're a good man, a loving uncle and brother and a loyal friend. That's enough for me."

He hesitated, and she pressed her case. "We're adults, and we're heading into this with our eyes open. No promises and no commitments, if that's what's stopping you. Just really great sex." She aimed a pointed glance at the arousal straining his zipper.

"Besides, if you don't get some relief soon, you're liable to explode," she teased.

His mouth quirked. "There are ways to take care of that. Believe me, I know." He sobered. "You're not a 'just sex' woman, Cinnamon."

"Oh, no? Why do you think I left my last job?"

Not wanting to share the sordid past, she wished she'd kept her mouth shut. But she had Nick's full attention. If talking about what happened helped convince him to make love with her, the story was worth the telling.

That didn't mean she could look at him while she told it. "Dwight Sabin, a founding partner of Sabin and Howe, was separated from his wife." She picked a feather from the down quilt. "We had an affair. Then he went back to her," she finished, leaving out the rest. "So you see, I know about sex without commitment."

There, it was out. She pulled in a fortifying breath before meeting his gaze. "Now you know my dirty little secret."

For one long moment she thought she'd convinced him. A tender warmth filled his face, and he brushed the bangs from her forehead. "So that's why you resigned. Were you in love with this guy?"

Fran had asked the same question, and Cinnamon replied with the same answer. "I thought so, but now I realize I was flattered. To have an important man like Dwight Sabin interested in me gave me quite a heady feeling." She sighed. "Until people started talking about me as if I'd lured him into bed and schemed to destroy his marriage, all for a promotion…." The indignity of it hit her in the stomach and she winced. "I couldn't stay there."

"I'm real sorry for what happened to you, but that story confirms the truth—you need more from a man than sex." Cupping her shoulder, Nick squeezed gently. "If I could, I'd deck the bastard for hurting you that way. Instead I'll just leave you alone, so I don't hurt you, too." He rose from the bed. "Tell Fran I'll be back next week, after the tourists clear out."

LYING IN BED THAT NIGHT, miserable and rock hard with need, Nick cursed himself six ways to Sunday. He'd had the chance to live his fantasies and make love with Cinnamon, and what had he done?

Turned her down.

You're a good man, a loving uncle and brother, and a loyal friend. That's enough for me.

He was flattered and pleased, but no fool. He was small potatoes, not high-powered enough for Cinnamon. She deserved a man who loved her and who could give her security and plenty of money. No way did Nick fit that bill.

She claimed she wanted him, but if she knew he could barely read, she'd change her mind real fast. Which would be best for both of them.

"So tell her and solve your problem," he grumbled into the darkness.

But he knew he never would. Truth of the matter was, he couldn't bear to see her pity; or worse, know that she thought him stupid.

Best thing for her was to hook up with a hotshot executive—as long as he didn't use her the way her jerk of a boss had.

From now on Nick would do his lusting for her in private. If it killed him he wouldn't touch her again. His groin pulsed painfully, and he groaned. It probably *would* kill him.

Swearing, and desperate to clear his brain, he turned to the only possible relief, dismal as it was. Self-gratification.

Chapter Thirteen

Thursday evening, having settled into the spare bedroom of Fran's apartment in the basement of the Oceanside, Cinnamon and Fran sat cross-legged on the guest bed, sharing a bowl of hot buttered popcorn.

Reaching for a napkin, Cinnamon wiped her lips. "Here we are, just like college." She glanced at her small but plush room. "Only, this is a whole lot nicer than a dorm room."

"But just as much fun." Fran swallowed a mouthful, then eyed Cinnamon thoughtfully. "So, what's bothering you?"

"How'd you know?"

"When your hands get restless, it's a sure sign something's on your mind. You're about to shred that poor napkin to bits."

"You know me too well." Laughing, Cinnamon lobbed the napkin into the rattan wastebasket a few feet away. "Not something, someone."

"Let me guess. Nick Mahoney."

Sobering, Cinnamon nodded.

"I take it yesterday didn't go so well?"

Thanks to Nick's excellent kissing skills and red-hot hands, she'd touched heaven, but that seemed too private to share, even with a best friend. "It was wonderful but also frustrating."

"I'm glad about the wonderful piece." Fran's eyes brightened. Good friend that she was, she didn't pry, simply offered an understanding nod. "Want to talk about it?"

How to admit that the man you wanted desperately refused to make love with you? Cinnamon toyed with the half-empty popcorn bowl. "He says there are things I don't know about him," she hedged with a shrug. "Whatever they are, they're powerful enough to keep us apart."

Fran's eyes narrowed thoughtfully. "Secrets, huh?" She shook her head. "This is the first I've heard of any."

"So, you don't know what he meant?" Cinnamon's spirits sank. "I hoped you did." She released a defeated sigh. "Well, I guess that's that."

"Not necessarily," Fran said with a gleam in her eyes. "There's always the Valentine's Day dance. Good music, champagne punch and romantic decorations." She fiddled pensively with the gold stud in her ear. "A sexy dress might help, and spiky 'love me' heels. Jamie's Boutique off Main Street is a good place to shop for both."

"I don't know," Cinnamon mused. "What if it doesn't work?"

"Then you still have a hot new outfit."

"Hmm…" She really shouldn't spend the money, but with the Boston job a definite possibility… She smiled at her friend. "I have that factory meeting tomorrow afternoon, and you'll be busy with your guests, so we can't shop then. We're meeting the Friday girls for an early lunch, so that leaves the morning. Interested in dress hunting first thing tomorrow?"

Fran grinned. "I certainly am."

SEATED AT THE USUAL big table at Rosy's late the following morning, Fran waited until the door closed behind Cinnamon before she gestured her friends forward. The restaurant was starting to fill up, and she had only a few minutes before she should head back to the Oceanside and wait for her guests, but this was important.

"Can you keep a secret?" she asked. All five women nodded and leaned forward expectantly. "Just for half an hour, until everybody at the Town Hall knows."

"So, this is about Cinnamon and the cranberry factory," Betsy mused, a valid assumption since that was where Cinnamon was headed for the buyout meeting.

Fran nodded. "And it's wonderful. Can I trust you

all to keep a secret?" she repeated, looking each woman in the eye.

Betsy pretended to turn a key over her lips. Claire and Lynn nodded solemnly, while Joelle and Noelle crossed their hearts.

About to clear the table, Rosy stopped. "Want me to come back in a minute?"

Fran shook her head. "You should hear this, too."

The restaurant owner signaled the other waitresses to take care of her station, then eagerly sat down in the chair Cinnamon had deserted.

"I spoke with the mayor this morning," Fran began, "and guess what? Tate agreed to the employee buyout. They're going to offer Cinnamon a job as general manager of the factory."

"Wahoo!" Rosy's fist shot into the air, Lynn and Claire echoing the gesture.

"Fabulous," Betsy agreed.

Joelle and Noelle smiled at each other in delight. "We would so love her to live here," they agreed in unison.

"I don't know if she'll take the job," Fran said. "What I do know is, she really likes Nick. Apparently he hasn't shown much interest. If we want her to stay, we've got to change that."

"What is he, blind?" Joelle said.

Betsy looked puzzled. "I saw how he looked at her at the town meeting last week. He's interested, all right. I thought— I mean, she said she didn't want him."

"Well, she changed her mind," Fran said. "Unfortunately, that hasn't changed Nick's behavior toward her. According to Cinnamon, he claims there are 'things' she doesn't know about him."

"Things?" Claire scratched her head.

"What things?" Rosy wondered. "Whatever they are, they can't be so bad. Nick is one of the nicest people I know. He's darn cute, too." She chuckled. "If I were Cinnamon's age, I'd be after him in a Cranberry second."

"Amen, sister," Claire agreed. Lynn nodded.

"Anyway," Fran said, "whatever these 'things' are, they've stopped any romance from developing. But take heart. Sharon phoned me a few days ago to discuss this very thing. She says even though Nick doesn't talk about Cinnamon, he definitely is attracted to and interested in her. Now—"

"Didn't I just say the same thing?" Betsy said.

Noelle tsked. "Will you let Fran finish?"

Joelle gestured at Fran to continue.

"Problem is," Fran went on, "Nick doesn't seem to realize his feelings. Sharon says he needs a push or two. That's where we come in. This morning I went shopping with Cinnamon for a dress and shoes for tomorrow night's dance. Wait'll you see the sexy things she bought. Her outfit should knock Nick's socks totally off. But we need something more."

The women were silent a moment, each pondering the situation.

"I know." Joelle brightened. "We'll ask the band to play lots of slow, romantic songs and make sure—"

"They dance together," Noelle finished.

"Keep the lights dim," Claire added. "That adds a romantic air to things."

Rosy nodded. "And the band should make each song last a long time. I can picture Cinnamon and Nick now, dancing slow and holding each other close…" She let out a romantic sigh.

"Be still my heart," Lynn murmured.

Everyone at the table nodded dreamily at the image.

"And don't let anybody cut in when they're dancing," Claire said.

"Or make sure some other good-looking guy goes after Cinnamon," Betsy said. "You know, to make Nick jealous."

"And then let Mother Nature take over." Noelle's mouth quirked suggestively.

With a wink, her twin nodded. "That's bound to work."

Fran beamed. "I knew we'd come up with something."

EVEN BEFORE CINNAMON reached the dining room for Saturday breakfast, she heard laughter and conversation from Fran's guests. They sounded happy, but with Fran's warmth and her good food, who wouldn't be?

Cinnamon wasn't as outgoing, but she *was* hungry. And besides, Fran expected her to eat with everyone. What Cinnamon badly wanted was to talk with her friend, whom she hadn't seen since lunch yesterday, about the surprising turns in her life. Not just the unexpected offer from the factory, but a call from the consulting company in Boston, offering her a high-salaried job. Now she could buy something at the Love on Main Street art show without guilt.

"Good morning, sleepy head." Fran beamed at Cinnamon. "This is Cinnamon Smith, the friend I've been telling you about," she said to the seven couples filling the table. "She came in too late last night to meet you then, because *she* was being wined and dined by our mayor and his wife. I got that in a voice mail message."

With barely a pause, Fran raised a brow at Cinnamon. "Since I had to get up at four to cook for you all, I haven't heard how that went, but you'll tell me later. Now for the introductions." Fran gestured to one side of the table, which she'd extended with extra leafs. "Cinnamon, meet Mitch Matthews, who has come every year for four years, and his lady friend, Carin Nelson. Next to them, Mark and Megan Holmberg, Stephanie and Jared Shurtliff, and Kirk and Elise Workman. Across from them, Jim and Sue

Robertson, who are celebrating their second Valentine's Day in the Orca suite, Jess Martin and Tina Johnson, who were here over the Fourth of July, and Bo and Carol Farmer." She blew out a breath. "Whew!"

Everyone laughed, Cinnamon included.

"Hi," Cinnamon said, taking the only empty seat beside attractive, thirtyish Sue Roberston. She gestured at the gulls on the railing outside. "Did Fran tell you about Stubby and Stumpy?"

"First thing this morning," Mitch replied. "Carin has flipped over them."

His female companion nodded. "Mitch mentioned the gulls, but I didn't realize how adorable they are."

"Don't I know that," Fran said as she brought Cinnamon a steaming mug of coffee. "The second batch of rolls will be out of the oven shortly. Meantime, help yourself to quiche, ham and bacon." Her eyes sparkled and she seemed to glow with happiness at the table filled with guests. "And of course, cranberry juice."

"We heard about that, too, and dutifully drank the stuff," Bo quipped, nodding at his empty glass.

While everyone ate and chatted, Cinnamon studied the couples around her. Maybe it was the soft classical music and cozy fire crackling in the great room, or the view, or Valentine's Day weekend, but each pair seemed engrossed in each other. Even the Holmbergs, who looked to be in their sixties. Everyone made polite conversation, but the intimate looks couples exchanged and the way they leaned into each other left no doubt about what was on each of their minds. Love and making love.

Cinnamon dropped her gaze to her place. As the only woman at the table without a partner, she definitely stuck out. That didn't mean she minded being alone. She didn't need a man to be content. In a show of independence she popped a forkful of quiche into her mouth, straightened her shoulders and held her chin high.

Yet she felt hollow inside. Maybe she didn't need a man, but she wanted one in particular. Nick Mahoney.

"Now that everyone is here, let me wish you a happy Valentine's Day," Fran said. "I hope you're all planning to stroll around the Love on Main Street outdoor art show sometime today because some of our local artists are selling some great stuff there. And please, come to the dance tonight. Both events are fun. Also—" she winked "—we serve great food at the dance."

Couples chuckled at that.

"We've gone to the art show and the dance twice now." Jim and Sue Robertson smiled at each other and linked hands. "Fran's right, both events are great. As a bonus, you get to meet some of the locals, which is interesting."

Fran nodded. "Tonight we're honoring Abby Mahoney, our star twelve-year-old, who won the Oregon State math bee in her age category. She lives right here in town."

While the guests talked about that phenomenon, Cinnamon thought about the evening ahead—and Nick. Yesterday Fran had helped her find a short, low-cut dress and sexy heels, but there was no guarantee he would notice. He could easily reject her.

That frustrating possibility loomed over her head like a dark rain cloud, and she considered staying in and reading a book instead. But she wanted to applaud Abby. And besides, if she accepted the job in Boston, this could be her last chance to seduce the man she wanted more than anything.

Sue tore her gaze from her husband to focus on Cinnamon. "Fran says you're a consultant," she said, while Jim continued to shower his wife with mooney-eyed love.

Envy sliced through Cinnamon. Would a man—Nick in particular—ever look at her that way? "That's right," she replied, picking at a slice of ham.

Across from her, Kirk and Elise Workman exchanged a brief, tender kiss that left her feeling even more bereft.

Why in the world had she sat down to breakfast with this group of lovers? Appetite ruined, she wondered how to leave without seeming rude.

"A very talented consultant," Fran added from the kitchen. "Over the past few weeks Cinnamon helped orchestrate an employee buyout of our cranberry factory that will save the company from going under."

"Really," Jim said respectfully, and even Kirk and Elise stopped snuggling to offer impressed murmurs.

Cinnamon gave a modest shrug. "I had plenty of help."

"Maybe so," Fran conceded as she brought the coffeepot in for refills. "But nothing would have happened without you. And that's not all," she said, topping off mugs. "Yesterday the factory offered her a job as general manager. Our whole town hopes she'll take it." She winked. "*That's* why the mayor and his wife treated her to dinner."

Cinnamon shot her big-mouth friend a how-dare-you-tell-these-strangers frown. Ignoring the censuring look, Fran returned the coffeepot to the kitchen.

"Are you thinking about taking the job?" Kirk asked.

Cinnamon, who had just popped a mouthful of quiche into her mouth, chewed slowly, giving herself time to form a reply. Of course, she loved the town, Fran and her new friends. The challenge of running the factory definitely excited her. The salary wasn't what she wanted, but the cost of living here wasn't as high as it was in a large city. Meanwhile, to compensate, the mayor had offered lots of perks, including an oceanfront, rent-to-own home. Then once the company prospered, her pay would go up accordingly, with bonuses, as well.

The one drawback was Nick. Lust aside, she was falling for him. That scared her half to death. He wasn't interested in settling down. Well, she wasn't sure she wanted that, either, not with Nick. At least, that was what she told herself.

Could she live in a place where she'd likely bump into him often, or would she be able to forget him and move on with her life? She longed to discuss her doubts with Fran, but with so many guests this weekend, a talk would have to wait, possibly for days.

She chased the quiche with a sip of coffee. "The offer came as a huge surprise. I'm flattered and definitely interested, but I haven't made up my mind." May as well tell the group and Fran about the other offer. "Funny thing is, I also got a job offer from a consulting group in Boston."

"Really?" Fran frowned. "You didn't tell me. Congratulations," she said with no enthusiasm.

"It happened late yesterday afternoon, and we haven't seen each other."

"I suppose you'll be taking that position."

Two weeks ago, Cinnamon would have answered 'yes' without hesitation. Now she sighed. "I honestly don't know yet. They're giving me a full week to make up my mind."

"Looks like you have some serious decisions to make," Bo observed.

Everyone at the table went silent, each person absorbing the information. The perfect opportunity to leave.

The oven timer buzzed. "The second batch of breakfast rolls is ready. Would anyone like seconds?"

"No, thank you," Cinnamon replied. She glanced out the window, where patches of blue sky were visible. "I think I'll take a beach walk and do some thinking. See you all later, I'm sure."

She cleared her plate and left.

STANDING NEAR THE TOWN HALL stage, Nick jerked at his tie, which felt uncomfortably tight. He hated dances, especially this one. He glanced from the hearts papering the walls to the red and purple garlands draped around the huge "Happy Valentine's Day" heart hanging over the town hall stage, to the band members underneath it, setting up.

Everybody in town was here tonight, including Curt Blanco, a photographer for the *Cranberry News Weekly*. He'd taken a few snaps of Abby for the paper, and no doubt wanted pictures of the dance for the same reason. There were people Nick had never seen before, the usual Valentine's Day tourists.

All of them were dressed in fancy clothes, including Cinnamon. A short, slinky red number hugged her curves, and high heels set off her sexy legs. Damned if that didn't wake up a certain part of his anatomy. She was killing him. The past three days he'd avoided her, and he meant to steer clear of her tonight, too.

After Abby accepted her award, he saw Cinnamon heading toward his niece. He slipped into the men's room.

By the time he came out she'd disappeared in the crowd. Now he combed the room for her but didn't see her. Catching himself, he frowned. Three days keeping his distance hadn't helped. He was still randy as hell and in a foul mood, to boot…proving that Out of Sight, Out of Mind was garbage.

He'd heard about both of her job offers. Everyone had. Which one would she take? If she stuck around here, he'd never get her out of his system. And now it was time to leave and take a long, cold shower.

"I'm out of here," he muttered to his sister.

Looking alarmed, she clasped his arm. "You can't go yet. You have to dance with Abby."

Nick eyed his niece, one of half a dozen twelve-year-old females talking animatedly and laughing nervously. From time to time they shot sly glances at the group of awkward, skinny boys hovering nearby.

Nick narrowed his eyes at the boys. If any of them so much as touched his niece… But since they looked scared half to death, he figured she was safe. "It's not me she wants to dance with," he grumbled.

Sharon laughed. "Well, then, stay and dance with me, so I don't look like a total misfit."

"Not gonna happen." Nick nodded toward the refreshment table. "Andy Jessup's been checking you out since he walked in."

"Has he?"

To his surprise his sister flushed. "You two have something going on?" he asked, arching his brows.

"Not yet, but I wouldn't mind. Look at Liz, over by the band."

Nick spotted her, hanging on some poor tourist's arm and batting her eyes.

"Looks as if she won't be bothering you tonight," Sharon observed.

He heaved a sigh of relief. "Thank God for small favors. Andy's not as bold as his older sister."

"That's okay." His sister fluffed her hair. "I think I'll get myself a cup of punch. Wish me luck."

Nick watched her go, and noted how Andy straightened his shoulders and smoothed down his hair. His sister and Andy. Nick shook his head. He'd never have guessed.

Ready to leave, he turned toward the exit. A sparkly red dress snagged his attention. *Cinnamon.* His body jumped to attention again. Damn.

She was standing near the exit, talking with Fran, Joelle, Noelle and Rosy. Meaning, he'd have to pass the whole nosy group on the way out. Scowling, he shoved his hands in his pockets and headed forward. Rosy saw him, and all the women waved. Before he reached them they melted into the crowd. Except for Cinnamon, who stood waiting.

Why that made him nervous was anybody's guess, and irritated the hell out of him.

"Hello," she smiled as he sauntered up. "I tried to say that earlier, but you disappeared."

Her curious look made him feel the need to explain. "Men's room." He shrugged. "Nice dress."

"Thank you. I like your slacks and sports coat, too."

Her eyes were warm and appreciative. Nick scrubbed his hand over the back of his neck. "Don't expect to see me this way again, because I only dress up for special occasions. I did this for Abby."

"Presenting her with a plaque and a savings bond was really nice of Cranberry," Cinnamon said.

"Sure was." He'd said his hellos, now he could leave. But in the silence that followed, he stayed put and searched for something to say. "That patent attorney called yesterday," he said at last. "She filed seven patents for me."

"Fantastic," Cinnamon said. "The cranberry factory should be paying you soon. I'm sure that's just the beginning."

Which would solve his worries about Abby's camp expenses. He grinned. "Thanks to you."

"You did the work," she replied with a modest dip of her head. "I only planted the idea."

The lights dimmed and the music started.

"Dance with me," he said, surprising himself.

"I'd like that." A nervous smile playing on her lips, she clasped his shoulder and offered him her free arm.

A slow, sultry song filled the room.

"That's not the way I dance." Nick wrapped his arms around her waist and pulled her close.

Cinnamon twined her arms around his neck. Her body pressed against him softly.

"That's better." Thanks to her high heels she was only a few inches shorter than he. Flowery perfume filled his senses. "You smell good," he said. She felt even better.

She smiled up at him. "Glad you like it."

"Everybody's talking about your two job offers. Which one are you going to take?"

"Everybody?" She shook her head. "News sure travels fast."

"That's Cranberry for you." Somebody bumped into him and he danced her toward the corner, where it was less crowded. "Nobody knows which job you'll take, though," he said, pulling back to look at her.

"I haven't made up my mind yet."

Her lips were fire-engine red, matching the dress, and he couldn't tear his eyes from them. He wanted badly to kiss her.

"I thought I'd make a list of pros and cons for each job," she was saying. "Then weigh and rank them, and then decide. What do you think?"

He was rock-hard now, and she must have felt it. He cleared his throat. "That sounds like something you'd do, all right."

"How would you decide?" she asked, shifting her hips close.

That one small movement nearly did him in. He knew then that he'd lost the battle. One signal from her and he'd take her home. This time he'd make love to her, consequences be damned.

Somebody tapped his shoulder. Nick turned his head to find Claude standing there.

"Mind if I cut in?" he asked, a sly look on his face. What was that about?

"Yeah, I do," Nick growled, pulling Cinnamon closer.

Claude shrugged and grinned. "Can't fault a man for trying." He jerked his chin at two other men from the factory. "Couple of my buddies want a chance to dance with Cinnamon."

Nick scowled at the men, who shifted nervously. "You're out of luck."

"I do like a man who knows what he wants," Cinnamon teased. "Guess what I want?" She flicked her tongue over her lips.

Have mercy. Nick barely stifled a groan. "Believe

me, that's all I can think of." He stared into her eyes. "But I don't want to hurt you the way that other guy did."

"The only way that'll happen is if you turn me down again." Her eyes were big and dark. "If that happens, I'm afraid I'll die."

Blood pounded in his head. "Wouldn't want that to happen." Bending low he placed his mouth against her ear. "Let's get out of here."

Chapter Fourteen

Nick pulled the truck into the carport and shut off the ignition. He opened the door and jumped from the cab. In the sudden silence Cinnamon's thudding heart seemed so loud she was sure the entire neighborhood heard it. Her body felt tight and sensitive, and her mind hummed so that she barely registered the yellow light over the porch or the small, fenced yard.

But as she opened her door, she heard the ocean and smelled the sea air. An instant later Nick grasped her waist and helped her out. She wrapped her arms around his neck as she slid down his solid body, holding him tight.

Groaning, he kissed her. Liquid heat raced through her body, and she returned the kiss with all the need inside her. A moment later he tore his mouth from hers.

"Not here," he breathed, grabbing her hand and pulling her up the stone walkway toward the door. His hands were cold, but so were hers.

A full, silvery moon peeked through the clouds and reflected brightly on the water. In a daze, she stared at the sight. "You never said you lived on the ocean."

"My place isn't much, just a cabin," he said, sounding apologetic.

"I don't care," Cinnamon said, and at the moment she didn't. Standing on the front step of the rustic cabin while Nick unlocked the door, she stared at the moon's reflection. "It's a beautiful setting."

Nick opened the door and turned to her. "You're beautiful. And I want you so much."

Cupping her face, he kissed her again. This time a sweet, nibbling kiss that left her panting for more. She parted her lips and tangled her tongue with his. His hand slipped under her coat and cupped her breast, and she wanted to melt right there on the step.

Just when her knees gave way, he pulled her inside. He kicked the door shut, at the same time tugging her coat off her shoulders. It landed on the sofa.

In the dim light of the table lamp she undid his tie and tossed it aside.

Nick unfastened his top button, then shrugged out of his sports coat and tossed it by her coat. Smiling into her eyes, he asked, "Where were we?"

Cinnamon placed his hand on her aching breast. "Here, I think."

He made a low, guttural sound and kissed her savagely.

She stepped out of her heels and hooked her foot around his calf—or tried. Her skirt was too tight for that. Breathing hard, she reached behind her to unzip the dress.

"Turn around and let me."

She did. His fingers shook as he pulled down the zipper. Or was she the one trembling? Feeling both excited and self-conscious, she pivoted slowly toward him.

The burning desire in Nick's eyes made her feel sexy and potent and her shyness dissolved. Licking her lips suggestively, she shimmied out of the dress, revealing a red lace bra and panties and thigh high stockings.

A purr of satisfaction rolled from his throat. "Have mercy."

"Not tonight," she teased, reaching for him.

Expression both intense and tender, he bent down and suckled her nipple through the lace. Waves of pleasure rolled through her, and her bones lost their strength.

"I'm about to keel over," she murmured.

"Can't have that. Bedroom's this way."

Nick jerked her toward a narrow hallway. They didn't get very far before he stopped to kiss her passionately. Each kiss, each touch, primed her for their joining. Along the way her bra disappeared, along with Nick's shirt. Somewhere in the hallway he pushed her against the wall. His soft chest hair rasping over her swollen nipples felt like heaven. Cupping her bottom, he lifted her. She wrapped her thighs around his hips, and he thrust against her. A picture fell, crashing to the floor.

"Oh, dear," Cinnamon murmured against his mouth.

He didn't seem to notice or hear her. "Come on," he said, carrying her to the bedroom.

Light from the hall spilled into the otherwise dark room. She barely had time to note the Indian print bedspread before he ripped it off the neatly made bed. He peeled back the blankets and gently tumbled her onto the mattress.

"Sexy as those panties and hose are, they have to go," he said.

Cinnamon closed her eyes and savored the feel of his warm hands peeling off her stockings and panties.

The mattress dipped. Then he was kissing her face, her neck, her breasts, licking and suckling until she writhed under him.

"Like that, do you?"

She nodded wordlessly, and his mouth quirked.

"Just you wait," he said, trailing openmouthed kisses down her belly, moving lower and lower.

Aching with anticipation, Cinnamon trembled and caught her breath. Finally he reached the apex of her thighs.

"Open for me," he coaxed.

She did. Soft, whiskery kisses on her tender inner thighs prolonged the agony. Whimpering with need, she at last felt his hot breath on her pulsing nub of desire. Parting her folds, he tasted her. Pleasure spiraled through her, sending her higher and higher. Teetering on the edge of control, she pulled back.

"Stop," she said, breathless. "This time you're coming with me. Take off your pants and lie down on your back."

"Yes, ma'am." His eyes dark and intense, he complied.

He was as perfect as she'd imagined, all hard muscle. His need jutted out, huge and magnificent. Cinnamon cupped the taut, smooth shaft and stroked, as she'd longed to do forever.

A groan of need rumbled from Nick's chest, and he clasped her wrist. "Keep that up and I'll embarrass myself." He flipped her onto her back and poised himself over her.

Need pounded low in her belly. "Please, Nick," she begged, lifting her hips.

"Is this what you want?" He thrust into her.

Shuddering pleasure pulsed through her. "Oh, yes. That feels good." Body and soul focused on Nick, she gripped his hips with her thighs. "Again."

"Like this?" He plunged so deep she no longer knew where he ended and she began.

"Yes," she whispered.

He pulled out and drove home, then again, faster and harder. Suddenly the world disappeared in a climax so intense her whole body shook.

"Cinnamon," he cried, swiftly joining her.

When the world stopped spinning, she was sprawled beside him, her head on his chest and his hand on her hip. Under her ear his heart beat furiously, the fast but steady rhythm somehow reassuring. She felt warm and full, and for the first time in her life, whole.

She loved him, she realized. Nick had been right—she wasn't a "just sex" woman. Frightened by the intensity of her feelings, she struggled to untangle herself.

"Where you going?" Nuzzling her shoulder, he pulled her closer. "You are so hot."

Hot was fine, but he didn't want love, would run the other way if he even suspected. Well, he'd never know.

"You're not so bad yourself." Carefully masking her feelings, Cinnamon lifted her head to look at him and smiled in a performance worthy of an Oscar.

She ought to leave now, before she did something foolish and ruined everything by blurting out her feelings. She opened her mouth to tell him she wanted to go.

"I'm thinking," he said, his deep, brown eyes warm

and aware. "We ought to make love again, to see how we do the second time." His hand slipped between her legs.

Desire melted her resolve...and her common sense along with it. She could no more leave than stop breathing. She licked her lips, then nipped his taut nipple. "I like the way you think."

SATED AND AT PEACE, Nick nestled Cinnamon closer and kissed the top of her head. "The second time was every bit as hot as the first. We're great in bed."

"Mmm," she mumbled.

She was almost asleep. Drowsy himself, Nick adjusted the covers, then closed his eyes. He liked lying here with Cinnamon. He liked the smell of sex and woman and the feel of her soft behind under his palm.

Warm breath slipped from her lips, fanning his chest. Shifting, she looped her leg over his groin. Just like that he wanted her again.

He scoffed at his new arousal. And here he'd thought once or twice would get her out of his system. Instead he wanted her more than ever.

As if she'd heard his thoughts she kissed his chest. Chuckling softly, he slid his hand up to her breast.

She made that throaty sound he liked. "I love you," she whispered.

Scaring him spitless.

"No, you don't."

Pulling his arms and legs free, he sat up. Then turned on the bedside lamp, blinking in the stark light.

Looking every bit as scared, Cinnamon followed him up, pulling the covers with her. Resting against the headboard, she tucked the blanket under her armpits.

"I never meant to fall in love with you, but to-night..." The words trailed off, and her hands moved restlessly over the wool, smoothing it needlessly. "I wasn't going to say it, but I was half-asleep, and the words slipped out. I can't help how I feel, Nick, and I can't lie about it, either. I love you."

Dazzled by her statement, he basked in the knowledge for one bright moment. Until a voice in his head cautioned him. *Get real. She'd change her mind fast if she found out you can't read.* That hurt too much to think about.

He couldn't tell her, not now. Not ever.

"I'm not asking you to love me back," she said, her big, cinnamon-colored eyes looking straight into his soul.

That was a relief. Nick nodded. Unable to bear those searching eyes one more second, he jerked his attention to the clock on the bedside table. "It's two in the morning—time I took you back to the Oceanside."

He swung his legs over the bed and stood. Cinnamon's panties were on the floor, a vivid speck of red on the beige rug. Averting his eyes he tossed them onto the bed. Her bra and dress were someplace else—the living room or hall—so he stalked out, retrieved them both and brought them to her.

"Shouldn't we talk?" she asked, still holding the blanket.

"Nothing to say."

He turned his back while she dressed. Grabbed his boxers from the floor and stepped into them. Ignoring his dress slacks, he pulled clean jeans and a T-shirt from his dresser.

Fully clothed, he spun toward Cinnamon. "Let's go."

Perched on his bed, wearing her bra and panties but not the dress, arms folded, legs stretched in front of her and crossed at the ankle, she shook her head. "Not until you tell me what you're afraid of."

What in hell? "I'm not scared of anything." Which was a big, fat lie.

"Prove it," she taunted, eyes shrewdly narrowed. "Tell me what you're hiding."

With her jaw set in determination and the fiery glint in her eyes, any fool could see she wasn't going anyplace until she got some kind of explanation.

Suddenly tired, he sat down on the lone chair, well out of reach of the bed. Scrubbing his hand over his face, he searched for something that would get her off his case. Anything but the truth.

"You deserve better than me," he said at last. Which was God's honest truth.

For several long seconds she stared expectantly at him, wanting more. Well, she wasn't getting another word. Matching her body language he crossed his arms and set his jaw.

Finally she threw up her hands. "Never mind, Nick." She jerked the dress over her head. "Just take me home."

"DON'T GET ME WRONG," Fran told Cinnamon as she coaxed two smoldering logs into flames late Sunday afternoon. "I thoroughly enjoy taking care of my guests, but after all that work organizing and setting up for the art show and the dance, plus cooking for a full house, I'm glad they've gone."

Cinnamon agreed. "They were a nice group of people," she said, propping her sock-covered feet on the ottoman.

But after a restless night—what had been left of it—and a full day of silent brooding over last night's disaster with Nick, she was more than ready to confide in her friend.

"Every group is nice." Brushing her hands together, Fran moved from the fireplace to the love seat. With a sigh she sank onto the cushions. "Now, I'm ready to put up my feet, relax and wait for that pizza we ordered." She lifted her wineglass from the driftwood-top coffee table, sipped, and then leaned intently toward Cinnamon. "So keep the wine flowing and tell me *everything*."

No need to ask what she meant. Everyone from the clerk at the grocery to the recently departed guests seemed to know she'd gone home last night with Nick.

But nobody knew about her frustration or her broken heart.

She tasted her merlot, hoping the rich, smooth flavor would dull the pain. Holding the stem of the goblet, she bit her lip. "You won't tell anyone, right?"

"Have I ever betrayed a confidence?" Her friend tipped her glass in a toast and winked. "Mum's the word."

"It's not good," Cinnamon warned.

The anticipatory gleam faded from Fran's eyes. "You mean he's lousy in bed?"

The only thing to do was laugh, and Cinnamon did. "Actually, he's quite good."

And then some. Despite her broken heart, her well-loved body still purred with satisfaction.

"Then what's the trouble?"

Cinnamon stretched her toes toward the fire, savoring the warmth, and sipped more wine. "For starters, want to or not, I've fallen in love with him."

"That's wonderful!" Fran enthused. "But I thought you wanted an executive."

"I changed my mind. Not that it matters, since Nick isn't in love with me."

Her friend shot her an incredulous look. "After the

way he looked at you at the dance and refused to let anyone cut in, I find that hard to believe."

"Believe it."

How else to explain his less-than-thrilled reaction to her confession, followed by his unwillingness to talk? And if his desperation to get her out of his bed and his house didn't speak volumes…

"Here I thought Nick wasn't what I wanted. Instead, apparently, I'm not the woman for him." She mustered a cardboard smile. "The joke's on me."

Indignation bristled through Fran. "The man's clearly out of his mind," she said with heat. "I'd be happy to knock some sense into him for you. Just say the word."

"Please don't." Cinnamon shot her a warning frown. "He made his choice. I just wish he'd explain himself. He's hiding something, but he refuses to talk about it." She stared into the deep red liquid in her glass, as opaque as Nick's secrets.

"Foolish man." Picking up the half-empty wine bottle, Fran refilled both glasses. "I suppose this means you're leaning toward taking the job in Boston?"

Cinnamon nodded. "I love this town, and really was tempted to take the general manager's job. But now how can I? The possibility of running into Nick anytime, anywhere would be uncomfortable at best. Plus, I truly want to meet someone, get married and start a family. There aren't a lot of eligible males around here." Even if there were, the only man she wanted was Nick.

"Well, fudge." Fran blew out a defeated sigh. "The mayor and everyone else will truly be sorry to lose you. We all love you."

"Not everybody," Cinnamon said. "First thing tomorrow, I'm calling Boston to accept their offer."

Chapter Fifteen

Monday afternoon Sharon barged into the workshop behind Nick's bungalow without knocking. "I've been trying to reach you for hours," she said as he slid off the adjustable bar stool he'd converted to a workseat. "Where have you been?"

"Where do you think?" Scowling, he gestured at the machine parts spread on his worktable.

She gestured at the phone. "You could have answered my calls."

In no mood to see or talk with anyone, he'd unplugged it. "I've been too busy for that."

She gave a tense nod, her eyes upset and her face pale. Worry tightened his gut. "Did something happen to Abby? She was okay when I dropped her at school this morning."

"She's fine."

He heaved a relieved sigh. "Then what's the trouble?" he asked, pushing the stool toward his sister. The legs scraped unpleasantly, and he made a mental note to pick up some rubber tips.

Ignoring the invitation to sit down, she crossed her arms and leaned against the wall, between the pegged tool board and a bin of spare parts. "Did you know Cinnamon took the job in Boston?"

Since he'd kept to himself all day, he hadn't heard. "Did she?"

He sounded as calm as the sea when the tide was out, but he felt as if he'd been punched in the gut. Grabbing a broom from beside the lone window he began to sweep the concrete floor.

"She's leaving in a couple of days. Now who's going to run the factory? We need her." Sharon glared at him. "This is your fault, Nick."

"Mine?" He snorted, the broom kicking up sawdust and debris. "What in hell are you talking about?"

"At the dance Saturday night, you only had eyes for each other. You took her home after, and you both looked darned pleased with yourselves. Something must have happened, because you canceled Sunday dinner with Abby and me for no reason whatsoever. Then this morning, Cinnamon accepted a job across the country instead of the one she was offered right here in town. I don't like that, but it's a good job and she ought to be happy. Instead she hung around the factory all day, moping around and snapping at people. I'm no rocket scientist, but I'm not an idiot, either.

There's a definite connection between your rotten mood and hers."

While his sister eyed him, he pushed the mess into a neat pile. Cinnamon loved him, or thought she did. That was the connection, but he refused to go there.

"What did you do to her?" Sharon asked.

Made love twice—the best sex of his life. He grabbed the dustpan from the its place under the window. "That, big sister, is my business."

"Did you tell her how you feel about her?"

"Again, none of your business," he said as he swept the debris into the dustpan.

"You didn't say you love her?"

"Because I don't," he said, dumping the pan into the trash bin.

"Oh, yes you do. I'm your sister and I know you, Nick. You're crazy for this woman."

"Fat lot you know," he muttered, but he sounded uncertain even to his own ears.

He leaned the broom against the wall. "I like her," he conceded, returning the dustpan to its place, "but I'm not right for her."

"Ah." Understanding dawned on his sister's face, and she pushed away from the wall. "I get it. You're afraid to tell her about the dyslexia. It's not a big deal, Nick."

He narrowed his eyes in warning. "Easy to say, since you can read."

"So can you. It just takes longer."

He didn't have an answer to that, so he frowned. "You done lecturing me? 'Cause I have work to do."

His sister shook her head. "You're just going to let Cinnamon go, then?"

"Yep." But the thought of never seeing her again made him feel sick in his gut.

Sharon released an exasperated breath. "Then you're a thickheaded fool, Nick Mahoney."

You're a thickheaded fool. The words echoed in Nick's brain all night long.

After tossing and turning and fighting himself for hours, he'd realized she was right. He *was* thickheaded, and tired of hiding his secret. She was right about something else, too.

He was in love with Cinnamon.

Crazy, lifetime-together in love. Admitting the truth felt amazing. His heart was so full he thought it might burst from his chest if he didn't tell her. He would do that right away, before she left town, and ask her to stay. First, though, he would tell her *everything*.

At the thought, his stomach balled into a hard fist, and tension knotted his shoulders. But if this was going to work—and there were no guarantees about that—she had to know the truth.

Unable to rest or work, he prowled restlessly

through the house until six. Showered and shaved, he phoned his sister.

"What do you want, Nick?" she said, sounding testy.

He didn't blame her. "Sorry about yesterday."

He could almost see her forgiving shrug. "You can't help it if you're a bonehead."

"So now I'm thickheaded *and* boneheaded?" He chuckled. "Prepare to be shocked. You're right."

"Huh?"

Since her confusion kept her from pestering him with questions, he quickly moved on. "Can you get someone else to take Abby to school today?"

"That depends on your reasons."

He sucked in a calming breath that didn't do squat. "I'm going over to the Oceanside to talk to Cinnamon."

"At this hour?"

Nick frowned. "What happened to 'Good luck, Nick'?"

His sister chuckled. "Good luck, Nick. Only you don't need it. She loves you, brother. But up the odds by waiting an hour, okay?"

Exactly sixty minutes later, nervous as a kid about to read out loud in class, he strode up the steps of the Oceanside. Standing at the front door, he rolled his shoulders to relieve the tension. He couldn't have said whether it worked. Shifting, then bouncing on his toes, he knocked on the front door.

After what seemed a good long while, it opened. Still in her robe, Fran didn't hide her surprise. "Nick! Hello." She swung the door wide open. "Come in. I didn't expect to see you today, but I can dig up work for you." Her gaze roved from his sports coat to his dress slacks. "What are you doing in your dress clothes?"

"No work for me today," he said. "I'm here to see Cinnamon." He cleared his throat. "That is, if she's awake."

Fran nodded. "We've already eaten breakfast. She's upstairs, packing. She doesn't leave till the day after tomorrow, but you know how she is about organizing things."

"She's not going anyplace if I can help it."

Fran's jaw dropped. He headed upstairs, his heart in his throat.

CINNAMON'S DOOR WAS OPEN, but Nick hovered uncertainly outside. "Mind if I come in?"

She glanced up from the open suitcase on the unmade bed, surprise on her face. "If you want. You're all dressed up."

"We'll get to that in a minute." Closing the door behind him, he moved slowly into the room, which was filled with clothes and books.

Books she carried with her to read. Books he would never crack open.

She lifted one, hugging it to her chest. "What do you want?"

"Better sit down," he cautioned. "I have something to say."

After darting a nervous glance at the bed, she pushed aside the clothes piled on the chaise and sat there.

His legs were shaking so badly, his knees nearly crumpled. "I think I'll sit, too."

He pulled out the desk chair and seated himself behind the desk. Her laptop was there, so he placed it on the floor. Hands folded in her lap—not fidgeting, he noted—Cinnamon watched him, her expression both wary and hopeful.

That made things worse. Recalling his advice to Abby about focusing, he pulled in a fortifying breath. Then slowly exhaled. Another breath, and he forged ahead.

"The other night you said I was hiding something. I was." Though the top button of his shirt was open, his throat felt constricted. He stuck his fingers inside his collar and pulled on it. "This is a part of me nobody but Sharon knows about. Well, I'm tired of that."

Pausing, wishing he'd never come over, he shot Cinnamon a nervous glance. The love in her eyes encouraged him.

"I don't read so well. I have dyslexia," he blurted out, bracing for her shock.

The relieved look on her face surprised him.

"That's your big, dark secret?" At his nod, she smiled. "I thought maybe you'd been in prison or something."

"Not being able to read *is* a kind of prison," he said. "I barely made it through high school." He shifted uncomfortably on the hard wood seat. "Didn't finish until I was twenty years old."

"That must have been very painful," she said, not with pity, but with understanding.

"More than you'll ever know." Needing to see her eyes, he looked at her straight-on. "If you don't love me after all, I can accept that."

Her eyes widened as if she thought he was crazy. "Silly man, I didn't fall in love with you because I thought you could read. I fell in love with you because you're warm and thoughtful and you have a solid gold heart. And because you're smart."

"You're the smart one," he said. "You have a master's degree."

"You don't need an advanced degree to be smart, Nick. I never could invent things or fix machines the way you do. That takes brains."

He saw by her face that she meant what she said. Her belief in him made him feel good. Smart, even. That new and heady feeling gave him courage. The tension stiffening his muscles eased, and he relaxed some. "Then it doesn't bother you that I barely graduated high school?"

She shook her head, her eyes filled with love. "I care about *you,* not your education."

They stood at the same time.

"You wanted to know why I dressed up," he said as he moved toward her. "It's not every day you tell a woman you love her. I love you, Cinnamon."

"Oh, Nick." She stumbled over a shoe, righting herself.

"There you go again, tripping. You need me around to take you to Doc's." He grasped her hands. "Don't take that job in Boston. Stay here with me."

Her eyes filled.

Scared out of his wits, he studied her face. "That is, if you're okay with living in Cranberry. I guess I could move if—"

"I don't want to move," she said. "I love this town and my new friends. I love Fran. And I love you."

Pulling her close, he kissed her. Minutes later, he tore his mouth from hers.

"Maybe we should get married," he said, looking into her luminous eyes.

"Really? Yes!" Her whole face lit up before she went into planning mode. "Where's my Palm Pilot? I've got to call Boston and cancel, then contact the mayor, and—"

"That stuff can wait." Nick plucked her open suitcase from the bed. He led Cinnamon toward it.

"Right now, I want to make love with the woman I'm crazy about. The woman I'm going to marry."

And they did.

* * * * *

Watch for Ann Roth's next book set in Cranberry, Oregon, IT HAPPENED ONE WEDDING, coming soon from Harlequin American Romance.

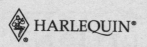

HARLEQUIN®

American **ROMANCE®**

COMING NEXT MONTH

#1121 THE WYOMING KID by Debbie Macomber
What do you get when you mix an ex-rodeo cowboy who is used to being *mobbed* by adoring fans, and a sweet schoolteacher who is *not* interested in him? For Lonnie Ellison, formerly the Wyoming Kid, Joy Fuller's lack of interest is infuriating—and very appealing. This could be a match made in heaven! *Don't miss this guest appearance by the beloved* New York Times *bestselling author!*

#1122 COWBOY M.D. by Pamela Britton
Alison Forester won't take no for an answer, especially not from Dr. Nicholas Sheppard, the renowned reconstructive surgeon. Ali's driven by personal reasons to make the new burn unit at her hospital a success. But Nick has issues of his own, and he'd rather patch up rodeo cowboys than join Ali. Even if she isn't your average hospital administrator.

#1123 TO CATCH A HUSBAND by Laura Marie Altom
U.S. Marshals
U.S. Marshal Charity Caldwell's biological clock is tick, tick, ticking away, but the man she's loved *forever* thinks of her as nothing more than a friend. Charity's about at her breaking point when she launches a plan to help Adam Logue think of her as more than a friend, and even more than a woman—it's a plan to make him see she'll be the perfect wife!

#1124 AARON UNDER CONSTRUCTION by Marin Thomas
The McKade Brothers
Life had been handed to Aaron McKade on a silver platter—until his grandfather dared the pampered heir to get his hands dirty and take a job building houses in the barrio of south central L.A. That's when he traded his Italian loafers for steel-toed boots—and found a boss lady with a tool belt to "rebuild" him....

www.eHarlequin.com

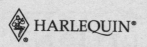

HARCNM0606

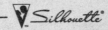

SPECIAL EDITION™

Welcome to Danbury Way—where nothing is as it seems...

Megan Schumacher has managed to maintain a low profile on Danbury Way by keeping the huge success of her graphics business a secret. But when a new client turns out to be a neighbor's sexy ex-husband, rumors of their developing romance quickly start to swirl.

THE RELUCTANT CINDERELLA

by CHRISTINE RIMMER

Available July 2006

Don't miss the first book from the Talk of the Neighborhood miniseries.

HOTEL MARCHAND

Four sisters.
A family legacy.
And someone is out to destroy it.

A captivating new limited continuity, launching June 2006

The most beautiful hotel in New Orleans,
and someone is out to destroy it. But mystery,
danger and some surprising family revelations
and discoveries won't stop the Marchand sisters
from protecting their birthright...
and finding love along the way.

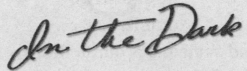

Page-turning drama...

Exotic, glamorous locations...

Intense emotion and passionate seduction...

Sheikhs, princes and billionaire tycoons...

This summer, may we suggest:

THE SHEIKH'S DISOBEDIENT BRIDE
by Jane Porter

On sale June.

AT THE GREEK TYCOON'S BIDDING
by Cathy Williams

On sale July.

THE ITALIAN MILLIONAIRE'S VIRGIN WIFE

On sale August.

With new titles to choose from every month,
discover a world of romance in our books written
by internationally bestselling authors.

HARLEQUIN® *Presents*

It's the ultimate in quality romance!

Available wherever Harlequin books are sold.

www.eHarlequin.com

HPGEN06

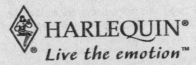